sleepwalking

Meg Wolitzer

RIVERHEAD BOOKS

New York

RIVERHEAD BOOKS
Published by the Penguin Group
Penguin Group (USA) LLC
375 Hudson Street, New York, New York 10014

USA • Canada • UK • Ireland • Australia • New Zealand • India • South Africa • China

penguin.com

A Penguin Random House Company

SLEEPWALKING

Avon Books mass market edition: April 1984
Riverhead trade paperback edition: April 2014
Riverhead trade paperback ISBN: 978-1-59463-313-3

PRINTED IN THE UNITED STATES OF AMERICA

10 9 8 7 6 5 4 3 2 1

Book design by Laura K. Corless

Praise for *The Interestings*

"*The Interestings* is warm, all-American, and acutely perceptive about the feelings and motivations of its characters, male and female, young and old, gay and straight; but it's also stealthily, unassumingly, and undeniably a novel of ideas."

—*The New York Times Book Review*

"A victory . . . *The Interestings* secures Wolitzer's place among the best novelists of her generation. . . . She's every bit as literary as Franzen or Eugenides. But the very human moments in her work hit you harder than the big ideas. This isn't women's fiction. It's everyone's." —*Entertainment Weekly (A)*

"I don't want to insult Meg Wolitzer by calling her sprawling, engrossing new novel, *The Interestings*, her most ambitious, because throughout her thirty-year career of turning out well-observed, often very funny books at a steady pace, I have no doubt she has always been ambitious. . . . But *The Interestings* is exactly the kind of book that literary sorts who talk about ambitious works . . . are talking about. . . . Wolitzer is almost crushingly insightful; she doesn't just mine the contemporary mind, she seems to invade it."

—*San Francisco Chronicle*

"A supremely engrossing, deeply knowing, genius-level enterprise . . . The novel is thick and thickly populated. And yet Wolitzer is brilliant at keeping the reader close by her side as she takes her story back and forth across time, in and out of multiple lives, and into the tangle of countless continuing, sometimes compromising, conversations." —*Chicago Tribune*

continued . . .

"Masterful, sweeping . . . frequently funny and always engaging . . . A story that feels real and true and more than fulfills the promise of the title. It is interesting, yes, but also moving, compelling, fascinating, and rewarding."   —*The Miami Herald*

"It's a ritual of childhood—that solemn vow never to lose touch, no matter what. And for six artsy teenagers whose lives unfold in Wolitzer's bighearted, ambitious new novel, the vow holds for almost four decades."   —*People*

"In probing the unpredictable relationship between early promise and success and the more dependable one between self-acceptance and happiness, Wolitzer's novel is not just a big book but a shrewd one."   —*The Christian Science Monitor*

"[*The Interestings*] soars, primarily because Wolitzer insists on taking our teenage selves seriously and, rather than coldly satirizing them, comes at them with warm humor and adult wisdom."   —*Elle*

"In Meg Wolitzer's lovely, wise *The Interestings*, Julie Jacobson begins the summer of '74 as an outsider at arts camp until she is accepted into a clique of teenagers with whom she forms a lifelong bond. Through well-tuned drama and compassionate humor, Wolitzer chronicles the living organism that is friendship, and arcs it over the course of more than thirty years."   —*O, The Oprah Magazine*

"Wonderful."   —*Vanity Fair*

"Juicy, perceptive and vividly written."   —NPR.org

"A sprawling, ambitious and often wistful novel."   —*USA Today*

"Smart, nuanced, and fun to read, in part because of the effervescent evocation of New York City from Watergate to today, in part because of the idiosyncratic authenticity of her characters."   —*The Daily Beast continued . . .*

"Wolitzer expertly teases out the socio-sexual power dynamics between men and women." —*Vanity Fair*

"Meg Wolitzer, like Tom Perrotta, is an author who makes you wonder why more people don't write perceptive, entertaining, unassuming novels about how and why ordinary people choose to make decisions about their lives. . . . *The Uncoupling* is a novel that can't help but make you think about your own relationship." —Nick Hornby in *The Believer*

"Every few years [Wolitzer] turns out a sparkling novel that manages to bring the shine back to big, tarnished issues of gender politics, such as women's pull between work and family, or the role of sexuality in family dynamics." —*San Francisco Chronicle*

"Superbly written, wry yet compassionate." —*ABC News*

Praise for *The Ten-Year Nap*

"About as real as it gets. A beautifully precise description of modern family life: the compromises, the peculiarities, the questions, the reconciliations to fate and necessity . . . written with the author's trademark blend of tenderness and bite." —*Chicago Tribune*

"Vividly, satisfyingly real." —*Entertainment Weekly*

"Very entertaining. The tartly funny Wolitzer is a miniaturist who can nail a contemporary type, scene or artifact with deadeye accuracy." —*The New York Times*

"The ultimate peril is motherhood, loving someone more than you love yourself. Meg Wolitzer nails it with tenderness and wit." —*O, The Oprah Magazine*

"Everyone has an opinion about stay-at-home mothers. With her new novel, Meg Wolitzer has just one agenda—to tell the truth about their lives. An engrossing, juicy read." —*Salon*

"Wolitzer perfectly captures her women's resolve in the face of a dizzying array of conflicting loyalties. To whom does a woman owe her primary allegiance? Her children? Her mother? Her friends, spouse, community? God forbid, herself?" —*The Washington Post*

"Provocative . . . Wolitzer's intimate look into these women's subsequent quests for validation is both liberating and poignant, as she deftly explores the relationships among family, friends, husbands, and lovers that shape her heroine's views of their pasts and the uncertainties of the future." —*Elle*

"[Wolitzer's] smart, funny, and deeply provocative novel takes the lives of its women very seriously. . . . She follows the inner workings of the minds of a group of friends in hilarious detail without condescending or judging. . . . It's a marvelous jungle in there, especially when written with Meg Wolitzer's unsentimental compassion and wit." —*Minneapolis Star Tribune*

for my mother

They have blossomed from the lands of death,
These flowers which a long-wrought dream has poured.

ANTONIN ARTAUD, "Black Garden"

preface

When I was twenty-one years old and had just sold my first novel, *Sleepwalking*, I took the train down from college to New York City in order to have my first meeting with my editor. After I stepped onto the elevator at the publishing house, anxiously clutching the little cardboard box that contained my manuscript, a priest got on carrying an enormous manuscript, a huge thing of many hundreds of pages, all tied up with twine. He looked at me and said, "Do they know you're coming?" I said yes, they did. Then he said, proudly, "They don't know I'm coming!"

I sometimes think about this moment, which dates back not only to the start of my life as a writer, but also to a different era in publishing. Back then, in the early 1980s, fiction was experiencing a golden moment. Novels anchored by all kinds of voices were being celebrated, even ones that, if they were published today, would certainly be considered "small." I'm not entirely sure what "small" means, exactly, or its related adjective, "quiet," but I know enough to have a feeling that *Sleepwalking* could be aptly described using those two words. And yet I don't mean this as criticism. I feel a real tenderness and protectiveness toward this book, in part because it was my first, but also because of its hushed awareness and its lack of showiness. I wrote the book I wanted to write, and I wasn't particularly concerned with whether it would find an audience, or whether it would be "relatable," which is a concept that all writers have heard a lot about in the intervening years. I suppose it was written in a state of innocence and mild grandiosity. I am fortunate to have a mother who was supportive of my endeavors from the start. Hilma Wolitzer, herself a novelist and the dedicatee of this novel, always pointed me toward good books and encouraged me deeply. We both loved the same kind of writing, and though I couldn't say exactly why I loved what I loved, I started to be able to recognize when a line of prose was good, and when one was a lot less good. I wrote *Sleepwalking* in the same way I'd written short stories for my creative writing workshops in college—with an eye toward language and observation much more than toward the overarching "thing" itself.

My novel predates the Brat Pack era that would follow it in a couple of years; this book does not feature a college world or postcollege world of careless debauchery, but instead one of bookish, brooding self-consciousness. I don't think the publisher quite knew what to do with it; the reviews were excellent, and yet when it was time to put out the paperback, it was decided that it would be published as if it were Young Adult, with a sort of lurid dark illustration on the cover of a pale girl holding blood-red roses.

People have asked me, smirking, about that cover over the years, and I've always hated to talk about it. The kind of book that cover seemed to suggest was contained within is not the kind of book I wrote.

I was struck by the YA/adult book distinction and overlap recently, when I published my newest novel, *The Interestings,* a full thirty years after *Sleepwalking.* Like my first novel, this recent book has a group of adolescents at its core, and it takes their lives seriously and hasn't been considered YA. I suspect that some of the ideas about teenagers in *Sleepwalking,* and coming into one's own, and being awfully self-conscious in the way that people can be when they're young, are still being worked through in my writing. For all I know, I've blithely plagiarized myself, and certain images appear in *Sleepwalking* that I later recycled. My recent work may be much bigger, literally as well as figuratively, with many more characters showing up, multiple points of view, a huge sweep of time passing, and certainly more plot to speak of, and yet, even taking a quick peek at the prose in the pages that follow, it's obvious to me that the person who wrote *Sleepwalking* is the person who went on to write her later novels. Although this person, in her current incarnation, would never let a publisher put a depressed-looking girl holding roses on the cover of this novel.

—Meg Wolitzer, October 2013

sleepwalking

Part 1

They talked about death as if it were a country in Europe. They made it seem that, after a brief vacation there, you could simply fly home bearing rolls of color film and tourist anecdotes. The three of them stayed up every night, usually until five o'clock, with the shade up and the window propped wide open, partly so the constant rush of air would keep them awake, and partly so they could observe the first paling of the sky, and pride themselves on how Spartan they were for requiring so little sleep.

Anyone who passed by the room very late on the way to the toilet would notice the slit of light under the door, would hear the thrum of voices from inside, sounding like a long, elaborate incantation, and would think, The death girls are still at it.

They had not always been thought of as the death girls, but

no one could seem to remember who had initially made up the term. They were famous on the Swarthmore campus, and any one of them could easily be identified from several yards away by the clash of a winter-white face with a perennial black turtleneck. As freshmen they had banded together, apparently drawn to each other by the lure of some secret signal as unintelligible to everyone else as the pitch of a dog whistle is to human beings.

They themselves thought it odd that three people with such similar sensibilities could meet at one college. They became friends during Orientation week. Naomi was in the library early one morning, browsing through the modern poetry section. Laura showed up a few minutes later. The two of them just stood in the aisle and looked at each other, startled. They were dressed exactly alike. Both of them were reading volumes of criticism and taking notes. Finally Laura said, "Wow, you're really hardcore."

Naomi answered, "So are you."

Claire joined them the next day. She lived in Naomi's dormitory, but they had not yet spoken. At breakfast Naomi heard a few people talking about Claire—how her shelf was crammed with books of depressing women's poetry and how she spent all her time by herself, off in some dream world. One boy made a tasteless joke about dead women poets, but Naomi ignored him.

She met Claire later that afternoon in the bathroom. They were washing their faces at adjacent sinks, and they began to talk over the rushing of water. They spoke about how they liked to write and about how lonely they had felt the last few days. Laura sat with them at dinner that evening, and the three of them got along exceptionally well. There was an immediate rhythm to their conversation, a natural fast pace. They talked about poetry and suicide, each a little bewildered to see that other people shared her deepest feelings.

Soon they were spending all of their time together. At meals in the cafeteria they huddled over one of the round, sticky tables in the corner. If some aerial footage had been taken of the three of them at breakfast, the result would have been starfish-symmetrical, like the June Taylor Dancers in top form. They appeared to function only as a unit, completely insepa- rable, but that, it turned out, was not the case.

Each of the three death girls had her own special poet. Laura's was Anne Sexton, and Naomi's was Sylvia Plath. Each girl actually looked like her chosen poet, or at least tried to. There was Naomi, that tall, lean girl with bleached blond hair and charm bracelets and a green leather-bound journal that she carried with her everywhere. She was of average height, but it seemed as though she liked to pretend she was taller, as tall as Plath had been. She always looked down at a person during a conversation, as if she were towering above. And Laura, graceful, cool Laura with her whiskey voice and decid- edly suburban air, she looked like Anne Sexton in the photo- graph on the flap of one of her books—Sexton lounging gracefully in a chair in someone's backyard, lightly holding a cigarette between two fingers.

But Claire carried out the most convincing imitation of them all. There had been many photographs of the poet Lucy Ascher printed in the newspaper when she died two years earlier. In every one she looked like a raccoon in the jaws of a trap, a pale, startled young woman with made-up eyes. This was the exact look Claire strove for. Every morning she ringed her eyes heavily with kohl, then she darkened her mouth with gloss from a tiny pot, and finally she put on her perfume. She wore ambergris only, swabbing it liberally from a vial onto her wrists, onto the plane between her breasts and down the front of her neck as she threw her head back in front of the mirror. She was the only one of the death girls who wore perfume, and it was almost a basic part of her. Next to Claire, Naomi and Laura seemed to be missing a dimension.

One Wednesday in September they decided they would meet late that night and conduct a kind of informal poetry session. That was the way the marathon nights began. When the dark darkened, they convened in Naomi's room. Her roommate, an outgoing girl from Nevada, had met a boy at a mixer and was spending her nights with him, so the death girls had complete privacy.

"I brought this," said Laura, holding out a bayberry candle. "I thought it would add atmosphere." Naomi found matches and lit it, then turned off the bright overhead light. She placed the candle on the floor in the middle of the room, and the three of them sat down in an awkward circle.

"Well, who wants to start?" Naomi asked.

"I do," said Claire in a soft voice. She opened her copy of Lucy Ascher's *Dreams and Other Living Things* and smoothed down the page. She was nervous, and her voice quavered during the first several lines she read. The room was dim and warm, and after a while she seemed to relax. Her voice rose up, sure of itself and of the words to the poem. Naomi and Laura had their eyes closed and were swaying slightly, as though they were being lulled into an easy trance.

This went on every evening. The death girls rushed through their days, impatient. They went to classes out of guilt only; the work hardly interested them. It was the nights that were exciting. The sun came down over the trees and the death girls started to wake, to come to life. "We're like vampires," Naomi said.

"Vampirellas," Laura corrected, and the three of them laughed a conspiratorial laugh, joyless.

Sometimes they indulged in a shared fantasy. They talked about the spirits of their poets communing in some special poets' heaven—they imagined their poets sitting on a dark, rolling bank of clouds, leading their own marathon session. None of the death girls seriously believed in the afterlife of the spirit; they just kidded about it. They all agreed that when you died, that was it, total stoppage. The thought of death swelled in them night after night.

There was a point that autumn when it got to be too much, when the thickness in the room was painful. By then it was a real habit, though, and it hurt to take a respite from it. Thanksgiving vacation came around—three days' release. In their separate homes the death girls sat in dining rooms with carved turkey slices on their plates and relatives crowding around, but they were restless. The world of their parents held nothing for them anymore, and they returned to Swarthmore eager and needful.

Once again they continued with their nighttime meetings.

Each evening was nearly a religious experience. The death girls would close their eyes and think of the suicides of their poets, of the sadness that filled every inch of space. Soon there would come that familiar odd rising feeling in each of them, and whoever's turn it was that particular night would begin to read the lines of a poem. Laura would always choose a different Sexton poem, but Naomi stuck with her favorite of Plath's, "Lady Lazarus." Claire usually read Lucy Ascher's "Of Gravity and Light," and although it was quite long, she knew the whole thing by heart. The air of the room was always rich with something new and inexplicable.

When it became light in the early hours of the morning, they would bring the meeting to a close. They would leave the dormitory and walk across the sleeping campus in a flock, feeling a unity they had never thought was possible. Death, usually such a divider, was the thing that held them together.

chapter one

He had heard she was unapproachable. "Talking to her is like talking to the Ice Queen," someone said, and he had no reason to doubt this, until the morning he actually did talk to her. It wasn't even a real conversation, but it was enough for him. Julian was standing at the water fountain in the library. He pressed his thumb down on the smooth metal button, then leaned over and curved his lips to catch the water that sprang up. It quickly filled his mouth and it was warm, disappointing. He swallowed, feeling a vague reminder of his elementary school days, when fountains were white and as low to the ground as urinals.

He stood and wiped spattered water from his chin. He realized, as he was about to turn, that there was someone behind him. He turned and walked away, barely looking. It was a woman in black; that was all he took in. Then something made him stop and watch her. He could see her shoulder blades as she stooped. With her arms jutted out and her head dipped she looked like a large, graceless bird about to attempt flight. He suddenly knew—she was one of the death girls.

It was strange to see her all alone. Where were the other two? he wondered. She had finished drinking now, and when she turned around he was still staring intently at her.

"Yes?" she said, in a small voice that surprised him. Somehow he had expected her voice to be deeper, more formidable. "Did you want something?" she asked him.

"No," said Julian quickly. "It was nothing."

"Oh," she said, blinked, looked uncertain and hurried away. She had been caught off-guard, and he, Julian, had done it. For the rest of the day he had visions of her large, dark eyes and the way they had blinked as though she were coming to the surface after a long sleep. She might well have been the Ice Queen, but at that moment she had looked bewildered. She needed to be in her trio; without the other two death girls she lost some of her grimness. He realized then that he wanted to touch her, and the newness of this idea excited him. Imagine: touching Claire Danziger, the deadliest of the death girls. He wondered if there was a softness to her somewhere underneath. If there was, he wanted to find it.

The next time he saw her, it was on the college green. While everyone else was lying in the sun, the death girls were crowded together, trying to fit into a single patch of shade cast by the bell tower. Julian was feeling brave; he left his game of Frisbee and sprinted lightly across the lawn. "Hey," he said, standing over the three of them. "Why are you in the shade? This is probably the last warm day until spring."

Claire's two friends barely looked at him. One of them was writing ardently in a green journal, and the other was reading a thick novel. Claire lifted her head, made a visor with the side of her hand and answered, "We hate the sun. We're mushrooms."

He smiled at her—his crooked smile that Cathy, his first lover, had told him was appealing. When Claire did not smile in return, it occurred to him suddenly that the death girls were probably without humor. After all, had he ever actually seen one of them smile? Their faces just weren't cut out for it. Claire's mouth, that fixed line, hardly moved when she spoke. It seemed as though it had been locked into her face that way for centuries, a fossil etched onto rock.

What she lacked in humor, though, she certainly made up for in drama. Two weeks later he lay in her bed for the first time and watched closely as she got ready for her morning lecture. He had awakened and forgotten where he was. Then he saw her sitting on the floor in the lotus position, already dressed for the day. He had spent the night with her; he could not get over it. He had pursued her, had asked people about her, and somehow things had fallen into place.

She stood up and stretched her arms out to the ceiling so that all her joints made little cracking noises. Then she shook her head back and forth and her dark hair fanned out and her long, hanging earrings swung against her cheeks.

She was late, and she left the room in a hurry, closing the

door hard behind her. Wind chimes collided lightly above the bed, exotic body lotions (avocado, sassafras) lined the surface of her bureau, and books were scattered about the room as if someone had broken in. As Julian lay there alone, swathed in leaky down comforters, he realized that he felt absolutely lost in her room, lost in her presence. Everything about Claire was an exaggeration, an indulgence. Whenever he was near her he wanted to lean into her, wanted to breathe her in. The evening before, when he was undressing in front of her, his penis sprang free like a joke snake in a can. After making love, he felt as though he hadn't climaxed, which he had. It was a vague irritation, like being at the beach and spending the day with loose crumbs of sand inside your bathing trunks. Claire was simply too much.

That night he tried to explain how overwhelmed he was. "You know," he said, "being with you is like being in a pie-eating contest."

He thought she would appreciate the cleverness and flattery in the metaphor, but instead she propped herself up on one elbow and said, "What's that supposed to mean? Sometimes you try and act so *sensitive* about everything, as if you're this innocent, earnest creature and everyone else out there is much stronger than you and much more prepared for life or something. You really enjoy striking poses, Julian. Who do you think you are—Young Werther?"

He was startled by her speech. He had never heard Claire sound angry before. "Talk about striking poses," he countered in a small voice, but he could not go on from there; he had nothing more to say. Whatever the battle was, she had won.

He often wondered what might entice someone into becoming a death girl. He knew that the three of them, Claire, Naomi and Laura, were not the only ones of their kind in the world. He had known girls who showed early warning signs in high school, at least at Dalton, which was the high school he went to—thin, faded girls who stayed once a week for meetings of the Metaphysics Club and who occasionally made comments in English class about the fine line between ecstasy and pain.

But this was different, far more serious, and he wanted to ask Claire about it, to find out everything. During the three weeks they had been together, Julian constantly feared he was drowning. Claire had come in and taken over everything. When he studied with her, he felt the need to look up from his work and watch her. She filled up rooms with her darkness, like a wave. Somehow it was a feeling he liked—gradually he was letting himself be carried along. He had learned to keep this feeling private. He was immensely careful when he was with Claire, not because she seemed breakable to him, the way his first lover had, but because he was afraid of disturbing anything, of irritating her. He moved slowly, cautious at all times, and each day he learned a bit more about what pleased her, and when to leave her alone.

One night they were sitting in the stacks of the library, way up in a remote wing on the top floor. The aisle lights had automatic timers, and every three minutes he had to stand up and turn the switch back on. There seemed to be no one else in this part of the building. He bet they could sleep there, right on the cool floor in the 800s, and no one would ever know. Claire was leaning back against a metal shelf, a book open in her lap. They had come to the library for its solitude only; neither of them needed any reference books. She had been underlining concepts in her reading with a yellow highlighter, and her fingers were dotted with color. Julian faced her across the aisle, and the stillness was awesome. It made him feel a need to whisper, as if they were sitting in a synagogue. "Claire," he said, "how did it start?" He did not have to explain himself; she would know what he meant. He wondered if he had done the wrong thing, if this would make her close up to him.

Instead Claire paused, shutting her eyes. "It's hard for me," she began. Her voice had dropped to the level of a whisper too.

"I know," Julian said, excited at seeing her uncertain, a little vulnerable. Suddenly the light shut itself off again. He started to get up and stopped himself. He found the dark comforting for some reason, and he knew that she thrived in it.

As they sat there, he could barely see the outline of her face, her hair, but their hands still touched; she was with him. "I don't know how it started," she said finally. "I guess I just sort of fell into it or something. Naomi and Laura, they say that it filled up their lives completely. I don't know if I feel that way. It just sort of happened; I wasn't looking for it or anything. High school was rough. The yearbook voted me 'Most Creative,' which was a polite way of saying they thought I was really weird."

Her voice was thickening, taking on a new texture. Julian could feel how painful all this was for her. Most people he had met at college spoke of their adolescence as a troubled time. Julian could not relate to this, although he often pretended to in conversation. It seemed somewhat inhuman for him to have actually loved those years, to have had an easy time of them. He had been good at most things, and what he was not good at, he faked. He was popular in the nonathletic way permitted only at small private schools. His family lived in New York in a brownstone on Seventy-first Street, and when his older brothers, Michael and Gabe, both left for college, he had the entire top floor to himself. Late at night he would lie on his bed, a book splayed open on his chest, listening to the Grateful Dead with his headphones on. Sometimes, he knew, his parents would come and stand in the doorway when they thought he had fallen asleep, marveling quietly at their gentle son. His mother and father loved him to the fullest, and he supposed that their love allowed him to live life easily, slowly. He was in no rush.

Claire had none of that quiet aura around her. Even when she slept, her hands were clenched into fists. This was one of the only times he had heard her speak in a soft voice, and it seemed ironic that there was no light, so that he could not see her face.

"I started with Woolf," she said, "which is what most people do, I think. She's an easy one to start with, because when you're fifteen or so you have this kind of romantic outlook on the world. I remember how neat I used to think it was—the whole idea of her death. I realize that sounds callous and horrible now, but I used to have this vivid picture of her in my head, a real pastoral scene. You know, this beautiful, tragic

woman walking slowly through the English countryside and
down to the water. She just keeps walking, picking up stones
from the side of the road and dropping them into the deep
pockets in her skirt. I used to spend hours imagining the scene.

"When I got a little older, I somehow had the idea that
poetry was better than prose. Maybe it's because I only had the
patience to write poetry. Really bad stuff, of course. I was editor of my high school literary magazine, *Kaleidoscope*. I think
every high school literary magazine is named *Kaleidoscope*.
Anyway, I wrote poems about swelling tears of rain and a couple of haiku about Vietnam, even though the war had already
been over for a few years, and I took myself very seriously."

Her voice was even lower now, and she told him how her
aunt had given her a collection of Lucy Ascher's poetry for her
sixteenth birthday, and how the poems were the most moving
she had ever read. She spent several hours each day with the
book, and her parents began to worry. They wanted her to get
out more, to do things. It was summer, and she should be at
the beach, they said, not sitting indoors in front of the air
conditioner reading those depressing poems. It was not a question of wanting to stop, Claire explained. At that point it was
already too late, she simply could not close the book; she was
drawn to it with a pull she had never felt before. The poetry
dealt with being young and feeling separate from the world
and dreaming about death.

"Lucy Ascher wrote about everything I had ever thought
about," Claire said, "and she voiced these thoughts in an
entirely new way. I can't really explain it to you. Instead of
being a boring realist, like those poets who write about gray

afternoons with lukewarm tea on a shabby table and two people sitting there who were once lovers but now have nothing
left to say to each other, she did the most incredible thing—she
made death an actual landscape. I used to read those poems
the minute I woke up. The night before, I would select a poem
to be read in the morning, and I would put the book on my
night table with a leather bookmark tucked into the right place.
When I woke up I would slowly remember the poem waiting
for me, and I would open the book and read it lying there in
my bed, barely awake. I didn't even get up to brush my teeth
or pee or anything but just read the poem through, and it really
made me feel good.

"Then my parents decided that if I wasn't going to get out
and have fun, I would have to get out and go to work. First
they wanted me to get a job at a place like Burger King, but I
absolutely refused. So they arranged for me to be a senior
counselor at a local day camp that a friend of theirs ran. It was
the most hideous place—no pool or anything, just a giant
sprinkler for the kids to run under, and the crappiest equip-
ment you ever saw. There was a volleyball net that sagged to
the ground in the middle, and even the real uncoordinated
kids could manage to get the ball over to the other side. The
whole setup was awful. I got fired after a week, because I just
sat and read *Dreams and Other Living Things* to the kids in my
group, when they wanted to be playing Spud. After I got fired,
there was a lot of yelling going on in my house. My mother
said I was the laziest daughter she had ever seen, but I really
didn't care what she thought. I had the book; that was all that
mattered."

Claire took a breath and said, "This is the part that's pretty hard for me to talk about, so bear with me, okay?"

Julian nodded in the dark. He didn't want to interrupt her in any way. He listened as she told him of waking up on July 18, 1977, when she was sixteen, and going downstairs for breakfast, already fortified by her morning poetry ritual. Her mother sat at the kitchen table, waiting. There was the smell of cooking in the air—eggs and coffee and some kind of batter. Her mother had the *New York Times* spread open in front of her on the table. She looked up at Claire and said in an expressionless voice, "That poet of yours died yesterday morning. She drowned herself."

Claire remembered standing in the middle of the bright kitchen and feeling, suddenly, as though she needed to lean against something. She rested her back on the side of the refrigerator and said, "You're making that up."

Her mother led her to the table, sat her down on one of the yellow swivel chairs and showed her the newspaper account of Lucy Ascher's death. It was all there, including a recent photograph of the poet accepting an award from the University of Michigan. Someone had looped a large medal on a ribbon around her neck, and the silver caught the flash of the camera. It was the only thing in the picture that shone; Lucy Ascher's face was solemn and in shadow, and her dark dress hung loosely around her. "I realized then," Claire said, "that Lucy Ascher actually *lived* in her death landscape. In that photograph, she looked like she was in mourning for herself or something."

Claire's mother had gone to the stove and filled a plate with food. Pancakes were darkening on the griddle, and she lifted them off with a spatula and poured on thick lingonberry syrup. Claire could not eat; she told her mother the food smelled rancid. This, Claire believed, was the real beginning of things. Since that morning, everything had seemed different. Her senses reacted to sights and noises and touches and odors in a new way. It wasn't just breakfast—nothing smelled good anymore. When she woke in the morning, her teeth hurt, as though she had been grinding them together during the night. She was cold all the time and wore sweatshirts in August.

"This has got to stop," her mother said one day, entering Claire's room without knocking. "You've been feeling sorry for yourself for too long. Snap out of it. It's not as if somebody you knew died. I mean it, Claire."

Her mother took her shopping, dragged her through three malls in one day, made her try on clothes she did not want. "Here," her mother said, holding up a size-nine blouse in the Junior Jet-Set department of one store. "You can't go off to that fancy college with no clothes."

In the dressing room Claire looked at herself in the three-way mirror. From all angles she appeared dull, in shadow, like Lucy Ascher.

"How are you doing in there, hon?" the saleswoman called, poking her head over the top of the saloon-style doors. Claire did not answer. She moved closer to the center mirror, and her breath clouded a small piece of her reflection. Now she looked as though she were only partly there. Was this what Lucy Ascher felt, this tedious drifting away from things? Maybe she was fading a chunk at a time, so that every day something new would be lost—the ability to sneeze, or yawn, or even blink. Horses, she knew, were not able to vomit and often died after gorging themselves on grass. Or maybe everything in her would start to hurt, even the dead cells, her fingernails and hair.

When she was very young she had once sat perfectly still for an hour, to see if she could feel herself growing. Years later she told this to a boy in her geometry class, and he laughed and said in a mock-lewd voice, "Hey, baby, want to feel *me* growing?"

Claire stood unmoving in front of the mirror, waiting for some kind of perceptible change, even a shimmer. And she felt it, right there in the dressing room, with its rayon smell and its pin-studded carpet and the young girl across the way covering her breasts with crossed arms. Claire thought, This is what it means to be a half-life, and then she slipped further into shadow.

They left the library just before closing, walking in silence across the lawn. The grass was no longer springy. The earth was becoming hard-packed, and leaves clotted the gutters. They decided they would sleep apart that night; it had been Claire's idea, but Julian quickly agreed. He wanted to be able to think for a while. Back in his room, he realized he had missed it. The bed had not been slept in for many nights, and there was a fine settling of dust on the surfaces of furniture. Claire always refused to sleep there. "It looks like Chip and Ernie's room on *My Three Sons*," she said. But Julian liked his room's stripped, plain look, and he stretched out on the bed.

Claire had opened up to him the way he had wanted her

to, but nothing much had changed because of it. She was a bit less of an enigma now, but Julian felt even more overwhelmed than before. Claire was certainly a full-fledged death girl. She could have been elected president of the national organization of death girls, if there were such a thing. She had told him everything—at least the surface of everything—he wanted to know. He understood that there had to be something more underneath, but he did not want to press yet.

Their relationship had evolved so rapidly that it startled him. He was afraid of losing Claire before he got a real grasp on her. At first he had been in awe of Claire, stunned by her, but now he felt something more. He felt sorry for her. He wished he had known her when she was sixteen years old. He could have helped her, he thought. He would have turned her away from the night side of things. Like a good parent, he would have switched on every lamp in her room, pointing things out: See, this is not an image of death. It is only a chair with your cardigan draped over the back. See, this is not a death landscape. It is only your bedroom. Then he would have shut off the lamps and leaned over her bed. Sleep now, he would have said, his hand on her forehead, before tiptoeing out of her room.

chapter two

She always had to be near the window. As a child she would fake impending motion sickness to claim the window seat in the car, and on airplanes she would spend the entire flight with her face pressed up against the tiny, sealed-off square of light. It was not from curiosity; it was just that she needed to have a sense of the distancing of things. She had been sitting at the window the first day Julian walked past. Several yards beyond her dormitory he stopped and looked upward. He was, she later found out, actually trying to guess which window was hers. When he saw her, he quickly turned away. He had not been expecting to see her there, he explained weeks after; he had hoped only for some emblem of her—a cracked prism, maybe, or a sprawling, browning plant.

He looked back again, slowly, hopefully. After a moment

Claire leaned over and pushed the window up with both arms. "Hello," she said from above.

Julian shoved his hands deep into the pockets of his windbreaker. "Oh, hi," he said. "You probably have a lot of work, right? I should let you get back to whatever you were doing."

Claire had been reading Hegel by the window all morning, and the room seemed hot now, closed off. She looked down and he appeared eager, even appealing. He rocked back and forth on his heels, waiting. He had been looking at her oddly the past few days, scrutinizing her. First at the water fountain, then at the snack bar, and once at the bookstore. It flattered her and made her feel self-conscious. She was used to distant attention only—discreet yet obvious glances. There was always someone looking at the death girls from across a room whenever they went anywhere. This was different. Bright-eyed Julian, the graceful Frisbee player, was drawn to her. She wondered why.

He reminded her of her brother. She did not think of Seth very often anymore, but whenever she did, or whenever he came to her unsummoned in a dream, his face was blurred, the features melded together. It was that way with all people in her life who had died; she could not visualize any of them— not her brother, her favorite grandmother or her Aunt Sybil, who had been killed by lightning in Montana just six months earlier. So she could not tell if Julian actually looked like Seth, but, like Seth, he gave off an aura of fragility. She did not know if she trusted this quality in him. He almost seemed proud of it, the way he did nothing to hide his vulnerability from her—looking away and blushing slightly whenever they made eye contact, stammering as he stood under her window. Since Seth died five years earlier, Claire's family had become oriented toward strength. Her mother spooned heaping doses of lecithin and brewer's yeast into glasses of orange juice every morning and talked on and on about endurance and will.

Claire looked down at Julian, and he seemed small to her. His upturned face was hopeful, almost pleading. "Do you want to come up?" she asked.

He bounded up the stairs, and she could hear his clogs clattering all the way up to her floor. Julian was the first male she had known who wore clogs, and she thought they looked good. He tapped his fingers lightly on the door. She opened it, and he seemed about to bow as he came into the room. The two of them sat in silence for a while—she smoking, he picking at some loose threads in a small tear in his jeans, as if it were a scab. She was thinking about how close to each other they were sitting. Usually she backed away, almost automatically, when anyone came too close to her. She didn't mind Julian sitting there, though. He wasn't demanding anything of her; he seemed to want just to sit in her room.

"Are you taking Intro. Philosophy?" he asked her. "I saw you carrying the book."

"Yes," she said.

"Do you have Parnesi? I had him last year and he's great."

"No," Claire answered. "I have Stein."

"Oh," he said. "Did you get past the *Republic* yet? It seemed like we spent an eternity on it. God, the parable of the cave— I still have dreams about it. And all that 'Oh tell me, Glaucon,' stuff. It really starts to swamp you—you know what I mean? Wait until you reach the middle of the course and start reading about the nature of good and evil. I'll let you look at my old papers if you want, not that they're masterpieces."

She realized how hard Julian was trying to have a real rapport with her. She knew that if she was at all cold to him he would be shaken. He was handsome—slim and fair. He had that rural look, she thought: he seemed to be the type of person who would be content sitting on the front porch of a farmhouse all day, plucking a guitar and taking swigs of wine. Men who looked like that were always frightened of her, completely put off. They thought she was too abrasive, and so they stayed away. Julian, on the contrary, appeared to be fascinated, and this in turn fascinated her.

He left after an hour of halting, broken conversation. He asked, leaning against the doorframe as if, she thought, to make it look like an afterthought, whether he could come back and study with her the following day. She nodded and could tell he was elated. Claire returned to the window as he clattered back down the stairs. She let herself fantasize for a moment about putting her arms around someone like Julian. She had not had a lover in almost two years, and the prospect of touch suddenly interested her. She watched him as he walked away from her dormitory. Even from the back he looked like Seth.

For a week after Seth's funeral, Claire had sat up nights with her parents and her older sister, the four of them hunching over the round kitchen table, as frazzled and grubby as Van Gogh's Potato Eaters.

"In death there is a sharing," Rabbi Krinsky said at the

funeral. Claire wondered if her parents believed him. He was a sullen, brooding man who had been with the congregation only a few months.

"All I want to do," Seth said the day he came home from the hospital, "is get real high. Like I used to in high school, when Jimmy Katz and I went out behind the basketball courts during Phys. Ed., and did up two bowls of Acapulco Gold. Get me nice and high, Claire."

She remembered the day very well and her own fingers putting together a joint, clumsily and wetly. She was fourteen then and had done this only three times in her life. She scratched a match to the joint, and brother and sister smoked quietly until there was nothing left. Seth inhaled one last time; he seemed to be smoking his fingertips. Later, high, he said to her, "I just thought I saw things in black and white for a second. I guess that's the way dogs see. I wonder what they dream about—maybe visions of Milk Bones dancing over their heads." He giggled to himself.

It rained all that afternoon, and Claire could hear the tin buckets her father had placed in the leaky basement clank with water. It was warm and damp inside, like a sick child's vaporized room. The smoke and the rain and the August heat were soporifics; Seth lay down on the tweed couch, his eyes blinking slowly, like a lizard's. He was falling asleep. Good, Claire thought, good. She felt relieved when her brother was asleep. When he was awake there was that constant knowing look, the expression common to all martyrs—Iphigenia, walking barefoot up the incline, fire sprouting up around her ankles like chickweed, that same expression on her face: *I know, I know.* Claire could not bear that look. When Seth slept he was just like anyone else.

Claire had read in some magazine that you could never have a dream in which you actually die, because the impact of it would be too much of a shock to the system and would cause you, in real life, to have a coronary or a stroke or something equally fatal. The mind and the body, working together in glorious synchrony, drag you up from rock bottom of sleep, so that you twitch and blink into consciousness before your falling dream body has the opportunity to make contact with the pavement below, or before your drowning dream body has the opportunity to swell its lungs with dark salt water and sink slowly and finally into the deepest regions of the ocean. Not even Seth could die in a dream. The sleep psyche is as innocent as a child, as protective as a mother.

In the beginning, they filled vials with his blood. There was an entirely new vocabulary to be learned; its words were odd and vaguely familiar, in a tongue that seemed as artificial as Esperanto: *Basophil. Leukocyte. White count. Platelet.* Claire's mother recited them on the telephone, and the words jumbled together made Claire giddy as she listened. *Platelet*: a tiny piece of dinnerware used at Lilliputian banquets, easily mistaken for a chink of green bottle glass on a beach.

Seth's remission, that most desperate of furloughs, had ended. Her parents phoned her at Buck's Rock Camp, where she was spending the summer on scholarship, taking classes in batik-making. "I think you should come home early, if you possibly can," her mother said, and the long-distance connection crackled and spat as though to convey the urgency her words could not express.

Seth had slept heavily all that afternoon, and when he woke up there was a patina of sweat on his face and neck. "I'm so tired," he said, "and so stoned." He propped himself up on one elbow and smiled, patting the couch. "Come sit here." Claire sat down lightly. It was routine; every day she had visited him in the hospital she had sat on the edge of his high, wide bed, barely resting her weight on it, not wanting to change the balance of anything.

Seth looked up at her, his face flushed, his pupils as full as gourds. "I want to ask you something," he said.

"Go ahead."

"Are you afraid of me? I mean, I read in a book by that woman Elisabeth Kübler-Ross, that people are scared off by people with diseases because it reminds them of their own mortality and stuff."

He was wearing an old T-shirt and a pair of khaki shorts, and he looked as if he were made of balsa wood. His elbow knobs and knees jutted out in hard points, like the edges of furniture you catch yourself on over and over. Claire thought it was the saddest question ever asked. How could she possibly be frightened of him? You can be frightened of death, but not of doom. It was easy to tell the difference: death does not have arms and legs as hairless and pale as a chihuahua, or fingernails bitten down to tiny smiles.

"No," Claire said. "I'm not afraid of you."

She leaned into him then, in a way she had not done in a long time. Born two years earlier than she, Seth had never been a forceful older brother. Neighborhood brothers—lifeguards, varsity soccer stars—had bent down and lifted their younger sisters up into the air in one fell swoop, and Claire had always been envious. During games of Running Bases in the backyard, she would charge into Seth as hard as she could, only to feel him sway and give like a tarpaulin in a storm.

Now he hugged her tightly, pulling her down next to him. "Oh," he said, the word coming from somewhere deep in his throat. "Oh." First Claire thought there was only despair in his voice, the lowing of a cow being carted off to the marketplace, but then she realized, as he hugged her even tighter, that there was also need. Seth's arm curved around her and drew her smack up to him. They were both high; this was craziness. "Claire," he whispered, "I can't take it."

She understood, in that one terrible moment, that he was somehow depending on her. She shivered, thinking that if she were to squeeze him as hard as he was squeezing her, he would snap cleanly, split apart down some invisible seam.

Seth was going to die; this was something she couldn't change. She felt the magnitude of it then, and it made her ache. She had grown up thinking that it was good to be close to people. There were times when the two of them had had pillow fights, had played board games, had had their photographs taken in one of those little booths together, contorting their faces in different ways for every frame. She had always been told that this kind of closeness was good, and her parents were delighted that she and Seth were real friends. Most siblings seemed to hate each other. The older kid was often a dictator, the younger one a whiner. It had never been that way with Claire and Seth.

But now she wished desperately that they had never been close in the first place. Maybe that way she wouldn't be feeling so awful now, so sad. For the first time in her life she wanted to keep a certain distance from him. There was already a space there, the kind of wall that separates the sick from the healthy. She and Seth were pressed together but it was not enough, and never could be. There was dead air between them; she could feel it.

Seth brought his face up to hers and kissed her mouth, fully. His breath was as sweet as a baby's—too sweet, as though he had been eating sugar beets. She kissed him back then because it appeared to be her responsibility, her calling.

Claire had once seen a woman die. She was nine and spending the day in the city with her mother. They were buying Italian ices from a vendor on Seventh Avenue when it happened. The woman who had been before them on line took one lick of her cherry ice, then walked out into the afternoon traffic. For weeks afterward Claire would think, I could have told her to be careful. I could have offered to help her across the street. I could have done something.

In the core of the bystander there is always a false sense of power, of responsibility. There was nothing she could do—not a laying on of hands, nothing. She lay in her brother's arms, his heartbeat frantic, his frame like a kite, and she eased away from him gently, thinking, I cannot save you.

———

Claire did not tell Julian that he reminded her of her brother. In fact, she did not even tell him that she had ever had a brother. She told very few people, not because it especially pained her to talk about Seth, but because such confessions were always responded to with lowered eyes, murmured words and quick, sharp hand squeezes, all of which made Claire feel like a faker. In truth, she did not grieve for Seth. He had been dead for five years, and she could not even picture his face. No one in her family ever talked about him, so it was, she kept telling herself, as if she had made him up.

After the funeral that August, all of the relatives returned to the house. Someone had pushed back the furniture in the living room and replaced it with a circle of hard-backed bridge chairs. Claire had forgotten those chairs existed; the last time they had been used was when her mother had held a PTA meeting in the house several years before. The family was forced to weep sitting up straight; they were no longer allowed the spineless posturing of grief.

Claire could not remember what it felt like to mourn. One time when she was home on Long Island for Christmas vacation freshman year, she stopped by the local King Kullen to see an old friend who worked there as a checker. Claire and Joanne had been friends the year Seth died. It was a mindless friendship, really; they passed notes back and forth during Social Studies and spent Friday nights at Burger King, giggling at people in other booths. The one remarkable trait that Joanne possessed was her ability to remember details, no matter how slight. Nothing went past her.

After Claire left for Swarthmore, she and Joanne saw each other only once or twice a year, and when they did it was only because Claire had some questions she knew Joanne could answer.

"What can I do for you this time?" Joanne asked her as she packed up an old man's groceries. Claire watched as each item was hurried into the brown bag: a tin of cat food, a package of luncheon meat, a single can of Diet Sprite—the man lived alone.

It must be depressing, Claire thought, to work in a supermarket. The foods people selected told a great deal about their lives, about the emptiness of their lives. This probably never occurred to Joanne, though. "It's just a job," she said once. "I never think when I'm at the supermarket." She smiled at all of her customers, and she sometimes hummed as she worked.

Claire sat down on the edge of the express counter. "I want to know what I wore to my brother's funeral," she said, running her hand along the conveyor belt. "I thought you might remember."

Joanne thought about this as she rang up a woman's purchases. "Twelve forty-nine," she said. "You wore that maroon dress with the little flowers around the edge." She did not appear to find the question at all odd. She was very proud of her ability to remember things.

"Did I cry a lot that day?" Claire asked.

"No," Joanne said. "You were pretty quiet. You didn't cry half as much as your parents did. That aunt of yours, I think her name was Maddy, or something with an *M*, whispered to one of your other relatives that you were probably in shock."

Claire had hoped that such details would help her recall what it felt like to be in mourning for Seth, but they didn't. She questioned Joanne for half an hour. When she could think of nothing more to ask, she thanked her, wished her a merry Christmas and walked out through the magically parting doors of the supermarket.

The only kind of grief Claire could remember feeling was her grief for Lucy Ascher. She had mourned the poet's death for months; in fact, she had never completely stopped mourning. Every day when Claire woke up, she thought of her. Ascher's face appeared out of nowhere, mouthing the words to one of her poems. Claire had tried to explain the whole phenomenon to Julian that evening in the stacks of the library. She told him more than she had planned to, and he listened intently. But he could not possibly have understood, she thought later that night as she climbed under the covers of her bed. Even Naomi and Laura did not really understand, although they certainly came closer.

There had been a split between the three death girls lately. "It's because of that Julian person you spend all your time with," Laura said one day. "He's responsible for the way you've been drifting away from us. You never come to our late-night meetings anymore."

"We miss you," Naomi chimed in.

"I know, and I'm sorry," she said to them. "Things will change soon; don't worry."

Claire missed the frenzy of their nighttime meetings. She had not been thoroughly honest when she told Julian about them. It was surely a lot more than just candles and notebooks and conversations about poetry. It was not a literary salon, the way she had made it out to be. It was, she decided, nearly a spiritual experience. She had seen documentary films of Southern Baptist revival meetings and had been awed by the passion of the people—the way they shook, trembled, could barely contain their love for Jesus. That was exactly how she felt when she thought about Lucy Ascher.

She would close her eyes, sitting cross-legged on the hard floor of Naomi's room, and think, *Lucy, Lucy*, blotting out all else. Soon there would come an odd lifting feeling in her stomach, and she would begin to recite the lines of one of Ascher's poems. Claire's favorite was "Of Gravity and Light," which was from Ascher's first collection. Naomi and Laura would respectfully wait for her to finish, and then they would each take a turn.

Claire barely listened when the other poetry was being read. She had no real affinity for the works of either Sexton or Plath. They were too common, she felt, too accessible, too whiny. Ascher was more complex, more difficult to take, because her pain was up front. She emphasized the fact that simple existence was filled with nightmare, as if this were already generally understood. When she could no longer stand the pain of it, she took her life.

A year after Lucy Ascher died, her notebook was published under the title *Sleepwalking*, from the name of one of her early poems. The book received much attention; critics called it deadly and devastating and apocalyptic. Claire thought it was merely realistic. It chronicled a life far more truthfully and painfully than anything else Claire had read. It gradually became a cult book, as Plath's *Letters Home* had been. Unlike Plath, Lucy Ascher never planned to have her words read by anyone, and that, Claire thought, gave them a stark, exposed quality. The notebook had been fished up from the very back of the poet's dresser drawer, underneath piles of underwear and little sachet pillows. The original notebook had, her mother wrote in the introduction to the book, smelled of gardenias.

Claire often pictured Lucy sitting curled up in a corner of her room, scribbling in her notebook until the early hours of the morning. She wished she could have been there with her, peering over her shoulder, fetching her a brand-new pencil when the old one wore down into a tiny yellow wood chip from overuse.

She could not voice her feelings to Julian; he would not be able to follow them. He was so simple—it seemed that he required almost nothing to sate him. "What do you need in life?" she asked him once when they were together in her bed.

"Just you," he replied, cupping her breast for emphasis. She was not amused.

Julian stopped by her room every day for two weeks after the time she saw him from the window and invited him up. In the beginning they studied together, sitting close and not talking for long stretches. Sometimes they played endless rounds of Botticelli, a game in which one player has to guess the famous person the other player is thinking of. Julian gave her difficult ones: Judge Crater, Mrs. O'Leary, and once, to be witty, Roy G. Biv.

In the middle of studying one afternoon, Julian leaned over and lightly bumped into her. His forehead knocked against hers—he drew in a long breath and then kissed her. Claire was not surprised. She moved away from him, annoyed, and said, "Just wait a minute, will you?"

He apologized to her, blushing as he spoke, and picking once again at the widening tear in his pants leg. Neither of them said anything for a few minutes. She knew that he was waiting for her to do something—to speak, to breathe, to light a new cigarette. It was her turn. His mouth looked very soft, and she was moved by him. She wanted him to touch her; she knew that. With a slight sigh, Claire stood up in front of Julian, placing both hands on his shoulders. He was up in the next second, as if his shoulders were points of reflex, like the knees. They kissed, and she brought him closer to her, gathered him in.

When they slept together that evening, she wondered if his initial awkwardness had been an act. After all, hadn't he seemed just a shade too quivery to be real? When she ran her hands up his long thighs, he said in a voice rich with feeling, "Oh, Claire, you are just too much." He looked as if he were about to falter, to pass out beneath her, and yet at the same time a smile was spreading on his face. Julian was clearly enjoying himself.

In the morning she woke to find him lying flat on his back, his mouth dropped open—a remnant, he told her when she questioned him, of mild childhood asthma. She was once again reminded of Seth. Was it some hidden, protective instinct that attracted her to Julian? The men Claire had been involved with in the past were always older, coarser.

In the twelfth grade she had met a twenty-four-year-old

man in Washington Square Park. She had been sitting by herself one Saturday on the lip of the fountain when someone slid over next to her. She looked up. The man was large and bearded and dark.

"Hi," he said, "I'm Rufus."

She introduced herself, to be polite, and he began to talk. He was a graduate film student at NYU, he said, and his favorite filmmaker was Jean-Luc Godard. Had she seen *Breathless*? Did she like to go to the movies?

Claire answered his questions shyly, then told him that she had things to do. "Oh, come *on*," he said, tilting his head to one side. "You don't really have to go if you don't want to. Come back to my apartment and I'll put on some good albums."

She went with him because she was feeling depressed and wanted a change, and also because the day was becoming cold and she couldn't bear the thought of going home just yet. Her father would pick her up at the station and they would sit in silence during the ride. He was unable to communicate with anyone; he sat at the breakfast table each day with the newspaper in front of his face. It had been like that for years.

Rufus lived in a tiny studio apartment near the park, way up on the seventh floor. As they climbed the last flight she told him, "This is the first real exercise I've had in weeks." He laughed excessively, as if she had just told him some terrific new joke, but actually she had been serious. She spent most of her days sitting cross-legged on her bed, reading Lucy Ascher's poems. She could not even remember the last time she had walked up a real flight of stairs. Her family's house was a split-level, but that didn't count. It was just four short steps to the safety and darkness of her bedroom.

"You're really funny, you know that?" he said, punching her softly on the arm.

The apartment was very messy, with cat hair on all the furniture, although there was no cat in evidence. Maybe, she thought giddily, he's the one who sheds. He did indeed have a lot of hair. After putting on a record, he confessed to her that he was not really a film student, that he had once been a film student but had been thrown out of graduate school for poor grades. "I had to hold down a job at Ray's Pizza, to pay my rent. I just couldn't do two things at once. Maybe someday I'll go back to school; I don't know. I still work at Ray's, but I think of myself as a student, you know? That's why I told you I was in school. It just popped out of my mouth."

After a while he asked her if she would like to drop a little acid. She paused, thinking she should say no and then get up and leave. She should thank him for his good music and for all the free cat hair which she would be taking home with her on her clothing. "I have to go," she said at last, walking toward the door.

"Oh, come *on*," he said once again.

She remembered a time when her parents were away and she came into Seth's room to find him and two friends sprawled out on the floor, laughing. "What's so funny?" Claire asked.

"We can't tell you," one of the friends said. "It's a secret." This brought forth more laughter.

"No, it's not a secret," Seth finally said. "Claire's okay." He looked at her with narrowed eyes. "Aren't you, Claire?"

"What's this all about?" she asked. "Be serious."

"We did some potent acid—Windowpane—and it's just starting to work. The walls are beginning to breathe; it's incredible," he said.

Seth had done a fair amount of hallucinogens in high school. He said that he was inspired by Carlos Castaneda. He and his friends went to see the movie *Fantasia* while on mescaline, and he told Claire that it was an absolutely amazing experience. "You know that part where they do 'A Night on Bald Mountain'?" he said. "It really freaked me out. I felt like my mind was being waked up for the very first time, each brain cell individually—like a million little alarm clocks were going off at once."

Claire had never tripped, although she had been curious about it. Rufus held a tab of acid in the palm of his hand, and after a moment she took it from him, and he smiled broadly. She stayed there the entire day, tripping like mad. The acid was called Blotter; it was a tiny snip of white paper with a greasy teardrop stain in the center, and she swallowed it at once so she would not have much time to think about it. It tasted like nothing, like a spitball.

She sat on his couch all afternoon, barely moving. The window shade slapped against the window, and a dog barked somewhere in the neighborhood. She fanned her hand before her eyes, looking calmly at the trails her fingers left in the air. Rufus put on the television set, and they both watched *Gilligan's Island* intently, as though it were a wonderful, important show on public television. When it grew dark outside, when the sky trembled into black, she left his apartment to catch the Long Island Railroad back home.

"Meet me in the park next Saturday," Rufus called after her. On the street, she had to blink several times to get her bearings, as though she had walked out of a dark movie theater into broad daylight.

Claire returned the next week, because she knew he would be excited to see her. She could tell he was very lonely, and she felt a kind of kinship with him. Two misfits. He was thrilled when she showed up, and as they walked to his apartment building he held her hand in his own huge, callused one. He seemed to have sprouted even more hair since the week before. He was wolflike—what was the word . . . lupine?—and this both repelled and excited her.

That afternoon Claire went to bed with him. She had never slept with anyone before, she told him as he opened up the couch. There were long, dark ovals of sweat underneath his arms, right where the seams of his shirt joined. He smelled of flour, she noticed, from working in the pizzeria. In bed Rufus was loud and rough, and when it was over, she was surprised that he had not hurt her in any way. She pressed her fingers gingerly against her thighs and abdomen, searching for tender areas, but she found none. I am a hardened woman, she thought.

Rufus brought over two flip-top cans of orange soda and lay back on the rumpled bed. He began to talk to her about a film he someday hoped to make. It would be a surrealistic Western, he explained, with all of the actors wearing white, featureless masks. "I'm positive I can get backers for it," he said. "Big money."

Claire took one sip of her soda and then said to him, "I've

got to leave now." It was as though she had just realized where she was and whom she was with. She put the can down on the night table and looked around her. The sheets no longer felt clean. They had the worn, rubbed-thin feel of cloth that might have been tangled through the arms and legs of scores of lovers. After the lovemaking was through, all of those couples might well have eaten boxes of cookies in bed, dropping little flurries of crumbs onto the sheets.

Claire gathered up her things, left the apartment and did not see him again. She stayed away from Washington Square Park.

There was one more after Rufus and before Julian. He was a swimming coach at the Y who always came to her right from the water, blue-lipped and eager. He had seemed to her amphibious. She wondered what it was she really wanted. All three of these men had looked bewildered when she left their beds, or rather, in the case of Julian, when she left her own bed. "I have to go now," she would say to each of them, shooing them away or fleeing herself. "Please."

Claire put on her make-up in front of Julian every morning. He was fascinated by the process and always sat up in bed to watch. She turned it into an elaborate routine for him, waving her stick of kohl in the air like a magic wand, and Julian was transfixed.

In bed he had said, "Tell me what you like," and while Claire was pleased by this, she had not known what to answer, because she had not especially liked anything in the past. When she first slept with Julian, their lovemaking was slow and painstaking. They reached for each other laboriously, as if through a fog. When Julian called out to her, insisted she was overwhelming him, Claire could not understand it. She felt annoyed, left out of the great secret. Julian touched her everywhere, slid his mouth down gently between her legs, and she thought to herself, This is fine, but that was the extent of it. She felt a welling up somewhere inside of her, but it was too far away, and she could not locate it. She did not know what was the matter.

Once when she had not responded to the swimming coach's ardent, chlorinated kisses, he had accused her of being without passion. She had believed his accusation without question. He was, after all, quite experienced sexually and had once made love underwater with a champion woman swimmer. They had gone through foreplay and intercourse, he swore, without ever having to come up for air.

Claire longed for real passion, the kind she had read about in romantic novels. She wanted to clasp Julian to her, to have their lovemaking be something new and exotic each time. She had seen that look on the faces of lovers in restaurants, on the street: a secret, meaningful glance exchanged between two people. There seemed to be a conspiracy of passion in the world.

To her, she had to admit, it was not much more than an abstract idea. The word conjured up images of fierceness: two lovers locked together as though they might never be pulled apart. She was fierce—she had that in her favor—but somehow she could not connect this quality in her with anything at all sexual.

The first day in seventh-grade hygiene class the teacher

stood up and said, "We are all animals." Everyone had laughed at this. The idea was new then, and it had seemed odd, embarrassing. Now it depressed Claire. On visits home she would occasionally run into people she had gone to school with, and she could see it in their eyes. Many of them were in love, or lust, and in that young-couple flush of desire and expectancy.

But Claire did not feel like an animal. When she slept with Julian her body was cool, straight, efficient. Smells and tastes did not lure her from sleep in the middle of the night. She had no fur, she had no heat.

chapter three

On Julian's birthday she bought him a red scarf. It was very long, and he wound it around the both of them. They stood in her room with their faces pressing hard against each other. He kissed her, and she could feel heat and dampness against the wool of the scarf. She was reminded of walking to school in winter, all wrapped up by her mother against the cold, breathing open-mouthed into cloth.

Claire liked giving presents. A year before Seth died she gave him an Etch-a-Sketch, a toy they had loved when they were little and had misplaced long ago. Somehow their coordination was off now, and they couldn't make any interesting designs. The box showed elaborate pictures of flowers and animals and sailboats. They turned the knobs for an hour, then gave up. "We were better at this when we were eight," Seth said. They put the toy away, and never used it again. It was still sitting in an old chest in the playroom.

No one had touched the toy chest since Seth died. It was big and made of stiff cardboard, with bright blue stars pasted all over it. Claire knew the contents without having to look inside. Every game stayed with her, and so did the memory of afternoons of play. There was benign Candyland with no words, just pictures of jaunty peppermint sticks and chocolate bars, and you moved your marker blithely around the game board, knowing that nothing really bad could happen to you. There was Go to the Head of the Class, which only lasted a few months because the reams of questions got used up. Somewhere at the bottom there was Twister, and this offered the most focused memory of all. Their father had brought home the big flat Twister box one evening for no particular reason, but just as a surprise. This was uncharacteristic of him, but Claire did not say anything. She watched as her father spread out the vinyl mat on the living-room rug. It had a vaguely unpleasant odor to it, like a bed-wetter's rubber sheet. Still, she was excited. Even their mother agreed to play, in the capacity of referee and spinner. *Left hand red, right foot green.* Directions were called, and soon they were a family tangled up. Claire wrapped her arms around her father's waist to touch a distant green circle. She was on all fours, and Seth was wedged beneath her, squirming. Her mother gave the spinner a good flick and called out, "Left foot yellow!"

The three of them slowly toppled in a heap, like the fall of an ancient, crumbling building. Claire lay there, breathing hard, her arms and legs mixed up with everyone else's. She had wondered how she would ever be able to grow up and move away from home, like her sister Joan, who went to college in Arizona. There was so much to connect people in a family; even if you weren't close, you still had shared histories. How could you ever leave?

"I can't bear to come East," Joan said over the telephone. "I'm doing such good work here, and I have a whole new life." But there had been one time when Claire had felt very close to her. Joan was home for a rare Christmas-vacation visit. The two sisters sat in the bathroom, in front of the big wall mirror, and Joan set Claire's hair with pink curlers. "Wait until Mom sees," Joan said. "She won't even recognize you."

Claire giggled at the excitement of this new allegiance and then sat quietly as her sister's hands, damp with setting gel, moved slowly through her hair, parting it and rolling it close to her head. Claire felt a swell of love for Joan, and she knew why: you love the people who take care of you. She closed her eyes and felt like a patient dog being petted over and over on its sleek, waiting head.

No one had really taken care of her since then. Julian tried, but it just wasn't right. She felt his bewilderment and inexperience, and she thought that he could barely manage to take care of himself, let alone her. She did not need what he wanted to give.

"Please don't touch me now," she said once when he reached for her, because she knew he would make it seem like concern, but it was really only longing. He could get an erection in about three seconds; once she kidded him about this and he became quiet and embarrassed, so she stopped.

Although they made love quite often and were serious about most things, she felt especially young when she was with him. Perhaps this was because he reminded her of her childhood picture of Seth; she was not sure. She was confused about childhood now; there were wonderful memories left over, but they always made her sad when she started to recall them.

Her childhood seemed especially brief—Seth sprouted upward and then weakened, and childhood was over for Claire. The games were gone, stored away forever. Claire invited no one home; the house was like a mausoleum. Whenever she went to a friend's house, the girl's mother would ply her with cookies and look at her nervously. "How are your parents doing?" she would ask in a hushed voice. "I've been meaning to call." Claire would shrug and not know how to respond, and soon the woman would drift away.

Claire stopped seeing friends after school. She rode the bus home and let herself into the quiet house. At dinnertime she and her parents would converge at the table and eat in complete silence.

Sometimes Claire wondered if she was going crazy. How long could she stand the silence? she wondered. Wasn't there a punishment for disgraced cadets at West Point called the silent treatment? At night, in her room, she would conduct small conversations with herself to review her thoughts of the day. She would lie on her back in bed, staring up at the ceiling, and ask herself in a whisper, "What's new?"

"Nothing."

"How do you feel?"

"Terrible."

"Will it ever get any better?"

"I have no idea."

Then she would sleep, a heavy sleep packed with dreams. Seth stretched out an inviting arm toward her, and they walked together through turnstiles, revolving doors, anything that moved. She woke up dizzy each morning. It was still dark when she went downstairs and made herself breakfast. Her junior high school was overcrowded and on a split-session program, so the ninth graders started their morning very early. As she rode the bus, the town was just waking up. Men like her father, who commuted into Manhattan every day, were warming up their cars for the long, solitary ride.

At lunch Claire sat alone and thought of Seth. She thought of his fingers—the way he could flip-flop a coin quickly through them, a skill that a magician at a birthday party had taught him. She could not get used to the stillness; that was the hardest part. Moving fingers, now still. Blinking eyes, now still, pale lashes shading nothing. And that voice—the hoarse hesitance of male adolescence, never knowing if it would split and jump an octave in the middle of a word. All of that, now still.

But then one night in bed she realized that it wasn't simply a matter of stillness. That was sad enough, but it also contained an element of the romantic: a sleeping prince frozen forever by a witch's spell. It wasn't stillness, she knew, and she sat up in bed. It was nothingness. Seth didn't even have a body any longer. There was nothing left to be still—some bone dust, maybe, and a suit of unfilled clothing.

Claire began to cry and could not make herself stop. It was the racking kind of sob; her body shook and she found herself gasping. She reached over and turned on the television set so that her parents wouldn't hear her. Johnny Carson came on, all brightness—white hair, wide clean smile. His guest was a blond actress in a sequined dress. It's as if our house is a private, sealed cave, Claire thought. Everything else goes on, even during this. The world did not stop for Seth's death. Traffic moved, school remained open. There were years of school ahead of her, years of waiting on long cafeteria lines and of getting picked for volleyball teams in gym class. How would she get through it all? she wondered. What would propel her?

Numbness would, it turned out. She found that through real concentration she could close out certain thoughts and focus only on the practical things. Parting her hair before the bathroom mirror, all she thought about was evenness, getting it just right. In geometry class she held her compass and swiveled it carefully over the page. A perfect arc formed, a useless bridge.

Then there was the Lucy Ascher thing. At least, that was what her mother called it. "What's this thing you have for that woman poet?" she asked Claire. *It is not a thing!* Claire wanted to scream. *It is everything; it is my life.* The earth split apart for Claire when she first read Lucy Ascher. Lucy Ascher seemed to say that we have a right to feel the sadness we feel. The world is bleak; the air is cold. Her poems were set in quiet places— the corners of dark rooms, the tops of lighthouses, empty bus stations late at night.

And then, after Claire knew it was all right to be depressed, to feel alone, she looked forward to the morning, to a new day of Lucy Ascher's poetry. Her parents stayed in the dim house and Claire rose above them, above it all.

It did not mean that she wasn't sad; she often was. The sadness stayed with her at college—at her side, a constant companion. Lately, since Julian, she had vivid flashes of Seth. He would be at the kitchen sink rinsing off an apple or sprawled out under a Japanese maple in the backyard, smoking a fat joint. Once she thought about Seth's bar mitzvah and pictured him standing up on the bema, embarrassed, the tallith draped around his neck as casually as a locker-room towel.

"Today, Seth Michael Danziger is a man," the rabbi had said; her parents made a recording of the whole ceremony. Claire remembered the words, and they were painful now that Seth was dead, and ironic, since he never really got to be a man, even though the rabbi said he did.

Claire found her father playing the tape once in the den, weeks after Seth died. She heard the high squeal of rewinding and then Seth's voice, muffled and slightly warped by the recording: "*V'nat tan lanuh et torah to . . .*"

She wanted to ask her father why he was doing this to himself, torturing himself in this way, but she was silent. He had the right to do what he wanted, to do anything he could to get by. It wasn't easy to stay in the present; Claire also had urges to move backward, to grasp things that weren't there any longer. She thought of it as time-tripping, what Billy Pilgrim did in *Slaughterhouse-Five*; her past would forge ahead by itself and she wouldn't even be stunned by it but would let it take over. Images poked up from their hiding places.

Oh, Seth. He had traveled around the country the summer before his death, sleeping out in campsites with his best friend, Mitchell, hitching rides from truckers. One night, he said, the truckdriver had been very tired and had asked Seth if he would drive for a few hours. Along Route 80, Seth steered the frozen-meat truck while Mitchell and the driver, a black man named Ramsay, slept soundly.

"It was really scary being so high up," Seth had told Claire. "Above everything, like God almost. I turned on the CB and all of these crazy people were talking, saying 'Breaker, breaker,' and everything. I drove until the sun came up. Then we stopped for breakfast at a Bob's Big Boy, and I just fell right to sleep with my head practically in my plate. Mitchell still teases me about it."

He had come home with a peeling sunburn and long hair. Claire ripped the thin scrolls of skin from his shoulders while he lay on his bed, electric guitar blasting from the stereo. She sat with him and made him tell her all about his trip. The summer had been so lonely for her—the first of many. The neighborhood was deserted; all the other kids were away at camp. Only the sprinklers made noise—that rhythmic stuttering coming from every front lawn.

She was getting real breasts—round swells under her blouse that she looked at for a long time each night. Seth got sick right in the middle of this. It was nearing the end of the season, and he was exhausted every day. One morning he came into the kitchen, rolled up his pants leg and said, "Look." There was a large green map of a bruise below his knee. It was painless, he said; he had just seen it there when he woke up.

And when they found out that he had leukemia and probably would not live very long, Claire continued to bloom absurdly. She looked at herself as she undressed for showers, for bed, and knew how useless it was. Such elaborate machinery, and what was it all for? Coils of dark pubic hair, widening hips. Her parents did not notice any of it; they were too involved with Seth, too frantic. He noticed, though. She was visiting him in the hospital, and as he lay on his bed he looked her over well and then said in a sarcastic voice, "So little Claire is finally becoming a woman."

"Shut up," she said, but she wasn't even annoyed. She felt like crying, and by tightening her voice she found that she could keep it in. Her parents had taken her out to a Cantonese restaurant the night before and told her about Seth. Even before that night, she somehow knew. She knew with a definite beat inside her, a weight dropping down.

Her father did the talking. He spoke in an even, gentle voice, and he sounded exhausted. Her mother just sat sipping tea, not saying anything. The restaurant was dark and empty; the only other people eating were two of the waiters on their dinner break.

"Dr. Marks said it doesn't look very good. He said we shouldn't be hopeful," her father said to her. She did not respond. "Do you understand what I'm telling you, Claire?" he asked.

She nodded but couldn't speak. Her mother continued to

pour tea for herself, finding something soothing in the warmth and the bitterness, Claire supposed. It all came down to this, to three people alone in a dark restaurant, defeated. Still, they continued to move through their lives. They grew older and left Seth fixed in his adolescence forever. They would remember him as a kid, not as a real adult. He had just started to come out of it, too, out of that "teen-age trance," as their mother liked to call it. He was waking up, thinking about life a bit more, sending away for college catalogues. And they had to leave him there, on the brink of everything.

At the funeral, people tossed dirt onto his casket. Someone handed her the small tin shovel; it was her turn. She thought of the dirt as an absurd gift, a final offering. She understood that nothing she could give him now would mean anything. She had read about people being buried along with their favorite books, foods, paintings. In ancient Egypt the pharaohs were entombed with their living slaves. Would she have gone with him? Would she have stopped her breath, given in to the dark, shared it with him? She did not think so.

There was no present you could give. She had always derived a good feeling from the act of giving, but she knew, really, that the act was twofold. A gift had to be received. Hands had to stretch out and take it, fumble with the ribbons and wrapping. Everyone was waiting for her now. She tossed a shovelful of earth down onto the coffin. It thudded and lightly dusted the surface.

chapter four

The summer Lucy Ascher stopped talking, the summer the words wouldn't come, she loved the crying and whispering of children in the night. She listened closely, the way an operagoer listens to a difficult aria: awed by those odd throat sounds she herself could not make. All around her there was noise—children choking on the bones of bad dreams, the girl a wall away who shouted "Fuck! Fuck! Fuck!" long into the night. In the background, like an accompaniment, there was the soft squeak of nurses' rubber heels on the aqua tiled floor, the clicking on of lights, the rush of tap water in a dented tin basin. It was all these noises, moving skyward like the smoke from many small fires and fusing together, that lullabied her nightly.

At the private psychiatric hospital where Lucy Ascher stayed one summer of her childhood, the grounds were tended as carefully as any historical tourist attraction—like the kind of mansion third graders are taken to on class trips, she wrote in her notebook. It was like the kind of place that rents out tiny tape recorders and earplugs so that you can wander around and hear a deep voice tell you about how Mrs. Roosevelt picked out the hummingbird wallpaper pattern herself, the kind of place where a curator leaves the train sets and chipped porcelain dolls of the President's children scattered randomly about the nursery as though the children had just abandoned their toys when called to the table for lunch. While her classmates, Lucy wrote, would be impressed by the high, lumpy beds and the heads of moose and deer that seemed to poke through the walls, she would be looking at Mrs. Roosevelt's wallpaper and realizing how yellow it had turned over the decades, like milk gone sour. "I would focus on decay rather than history," Lucy explained.

The hospital had a sweeping half-moon drive crunchy with gravel, and it was set far back from the road, "nestled in pine," as the catalogue read. Her parents sent away for hospital brochures as if they were looking into summer camps, and in the end this famous place was picked, right in the heart of the Berkshires. Her parents would go to Tanglewood in the evenings of their visits, stretching out side by side, defeated, on her father's old army blanket.

She had lost her ability to speak; it was as simple as that. Ten years later she went out with a man named Richard whose mother had had a stroke and would say, whenever her telephone rang, "Would somebody please answer the steeple?" "Telephone" was lost somewhere in the collapsed portion of her thinking—lost forever, a mitten, a shoe. Lost, but inexplicably replaced, and that was the difference between them. Lucy could not replace her words. "There was a seashell pressed indefinitely to my ear, and the sea-static terrified me. I was twelve years old, and one morning my mother found me curled in my room, late for school, trembling. 'Lucy,' she said, drying her hands on a dishtowel, 'are you sick, sweetie?' But I could not answer her; the rushing was too loud. I opened my mouth like a pathetic, newly hatched bird—opened and closed it, opened and closed it, gasping for air, gasping for words."

There should have been a drowning—one of her parents going under during a family boat outing. Maybe that would have been a reasonable excuse for the silence that was knitted so closely around her. There should have been a death of some kind, or at the very least a trauma. Perhaps her parents got angry and hit her sometimes, the young male psychologist suggested, leaning forward in his chair, springs straining. But she was clean—no suggestive purple bruises, no burn marks rippling up on her arms or the backs of her legs. There was no obvious explanation; her family life was intact. Her parents were very married. Her father sometimes stood behind her mother in the kitchen, placing his broad hands over her hips while she prepared dinner. "Ray," she would hiss, "stop it," but as she lifted the lid of a tureen of soup Lucy could still glimpse the quick light of her smile behind the rising steam.

Someone had led her out into the sun and placed an old *Richie Rich* comic book on her lap. She was sitting there by herself, her thoughts going nowhere, encircling her like a stupid dog in yipping pursuit of its tail, when she first met Levin. He walked slowly across the wide expanse of grass and pulled up a chair next to her. She guessed that he must have been close to thirty-five then, and she remembered that he was as thin and graceful as a praying mantis, and that he wore Italian leather sandals with black ankle socks.

Although the children's wing was separate from the rest of the hospital, the front lawn was common ground, and that day she had been placed on one of the mildewed canvas lawn chairs, a white oval of sun block centered on her nose, the work of a thoughtful nurse's aide. This was recreation hour, and all of the children sat unmoving on the lawn, as if in an extended game of Statues. Every day most of them drank little fluted cups of apple juice cloudy with Thorazine, and all their eyes were bright, their pupils huge. The taste of the apple juice stayed with her for years, "hitting me in the way that an old knee injury might ache during rainy season. I taste it at the back of my throat, the thick, phlegmy sweetness of it, and I also remember the nurse's encouraging smile and nod as I swallowed it all."

Being sedated, it turned out, did not loosen the roaring from her. All it did was make her less able to focus on it. Lucy still heard the roaring full-volume each day, the intangible sound of cars on a freeway, but she only had the energy to acknowledge its presence, and she became slowly used to it.

"Well," the man said, lowering himself carefully onto the chair as if into steaming bathwater, "you seem to be enjoying the sun." He took a pack of Kents from his shirt pocket and tapped out a single cigarette. "Smoke?" he asked, then laughed. "No, I guess you don't." He lit the cigarette with a narrow silver lighter and took several deep drags. Then he leaned back in his chair, closing his eyes. After a while he said, "I'm Reuben Levin. You're the one who doesn't speak, aren't you?" He laughed once more, gently. "That's like those horrible puzzles that ask you to find out which man is the liar. 'A' says he's not the liar, 'B' says 'A' is lying, et cetera. You have to figure out which man it is. So I guess if you don't answer me it's either because you just don't want to or because you really are the one who won't speak. I heard a few nurses talking about you, if it really is you."

He finished his cigarette, dropping the stub lightly on the grass. "It's supposed to grow into a cigarette tree now," he said, "like in that song 'Big Rock Candy Mountain.' We'll have to come back and check in a couple of years." He stood up suddenly, and she could see that his face had already begun to flush with sun. "It's much too hot out here," he said. "I'm going in." He leaned over then and kissed her high on her forehead, right where the middle part scalloped down into a widow's peak. "There," he said in a low voice. "It's been good talking with you."

The next time Lucy saw him she was with her parents in the solarium. The room's name was misleading; light came in modestly there, filtered through tinted glass. Everything was cool blue, like the diving section of a heavily chlorinated swimming pool. Her parents had brought along things she used to love to eat: long red licorice whips and packets of cocoa mix with tiny marshmallows that bloat when you pour in boiling water. "Look who's over there," her father said, poking her mother. He named an actor who had done a lot of specials for public television.

Her mother strained to see across the room, and after a moment she nodded. "Yes, I think you're right," she said. "I heard somewhere that he had a nervous breakdown, but I had no idea he was here." The actor was talking and laughing with visitors, but they did not interest Lucy. A few feet away, though, sat Levin, the man from the lawn, flanked by a woman and a small boy. The woman and the boy were doing all the talking, "their hands flying up around their heads like propellers as they spoke." Levin was sitting quietly, listening. Occasionally he said something, but for the most part he was silent. When visiting hours came to an end and the room shifted to a deeper blue, the woman threw her bangled arms around Levin's neck and whispered into his ear. The small boy hooked onto one of Levin's legs and stayed there, like an appendage.

In Occupational Therapy the children were stringing elbow macaroni into necklaces, and Lucy began to enjoy the rhythm of it, the clicking of piece upon piece. Someone was moaning across the table—a nine-year-old girl who had tried to hang herself with a jump rope in her bedroom at home. She sat helpless now, raw pasta and bits of glitter scattered in front of her, untouched. Lucy looked up and realized that Levin was standing in the doorway, watching her. Beverly, the occupational therapist, noticed him also.

"Hi, Mr. Levin," she said. "Can I do something for you? Do you want some more lanyard?"

"No," he said, an edge of sarcasm in his voice. "I still have yards to go. I came to talk to Lucy Ascher, if that's okay."

Beverly looked doubtful, but finally she agreed that he could come in for a little while. Levin sat down on one of the high, spindly stools. He was wearing a dark maroon bathrobe, and Lucy could see how slender and long his legs were. "I never really introduced myself to you," he said. "At least not formally. I only told you my name, nothing more. If we were in prison, I'd tell you what I was in for, like they did in that big prison movie. But this is almost the same thing, isn't it? I mean, we're all in here for *something*. I'll tell you one thing, though. I'm not paying for it. It turns out there's all this money lying around the university where I teach—a fund that helps tenured faculty pay for hospitalization. The last person who got to use the money was somebody three years ago. Cancer of the colon. He only used five weeks' worth, though, and you can pretty much guess the rest. So I'm doing time because I'm a wreck, because the counting man has gotten to me." He paused. "I suppose that sounds a little odd. You're young enough to know what I'm talking about   those cardboard figures that hold up their hands, and you learn how to subtract by breaking off their fingers at the knuckle, and you learn how to add by putting them back on. I'm sure you've seen them. As a kind of academic joke there's a counting man in the math department faculty lounge. People put funny hats on it or dress it up like a woman and put a lampshade on its head and dance with it at the big Christmas party and everyone laughs."

He continued speaking like this for almost half an hour, telling her how the presence of the counting man had given him the idea of counting things. He began counting squares of linoleum on the floor when he walked across a room, he counted the spines of books on every shelf he passed, he counted the moles, the beauty marks, that lightly dotted his wife's body. "Even you," he said, "you're wearing twenty buttons—twelve on your shirt including the pockets, and eight on your sweater. Useless information. See what I'm going through?"

His voice sounded good to her; it rose and fell in erratic slides like a calliope, and nobody had ever talked to Lucy at such length before. Levin stood up, looming over her. "You," he said in a whisper, "are the only one I've met who just *sits* there. I can't tell you what a pleasure it is."

Beverly came up behind them, her hand on Lucy's shoulder. "Lucy," she said, "please start cleaning up your things. O.T. is just about over for today."

Around the room, children were putting away their creations in designated cubbyholes or wiping the tabletops, or just sitting on their stools, feet hooked over the top rungs, rocking to a private music. One boy was eating paste from a gallon-sized jar. It was time to leave.

"Want to go out on the porch?" Levin asked. She deposited her macaroni necklace in the corner—her string of worry beads, her rosary—and they left the room together.

In my mute world even the dreams were voiceless," Lucy wrote, "populated by characters who ran around as silent and frantic as Keystone Kops. A nurse flashed a circle of light in my eyes late one night, lurching me from one of these dreams. 'You were shivering,' she explained to me, drawing the blanket up around my shoulders."

Summer was ending, and they were no longer taken outside

for recreation hour. Instead, everyone sat in the television room, old reruns blaring, the laughter of the children in front of the set strangely rapid and even, like machine-gun fire, after every gag line. Levin often came and sat with her, talking about his life, his teaching, his counting. He and his wife, Judith, lived in Connecticut and had one child. "I guess we have a pretty good life," he said. "At least we did until recently. Jason loves kindergarten, and Judith seems fairly happy most of the time. That night when she called up my friend Lew from the math department to come over and talk to me, I think she knew what I was going through and was really scared. She and Lew came into my study, where I'd been for twelve hours agonizing over numbers, and Lew told me I was doing this to myself and that he would help me. He said he would cover my nine o'clock section in the morning, and wasn't I teaching them eigenvalues now?"

Levin seemed to be building himself up to some kind of minor frenzy, and his words came out faster. "Judith asked if I wanted something to make me sleep, and I said yes, and she gave me something and then pulled out the Castro convertible in the study because I couldn't leave the room that night. This is the horrible part: all of a sudden Jason poked his head out through the slats of the banister; I guess the talking woke him, and Judith called to him in this really controlled voice, 'Go back to bed, baby. I'll be in to sing you our song about the windmills.' Then I realized that I didn't know what song she was talking about, and that I had been a negligent father and husband, and that my wife and child had a camaraderie I knew nothing about. It was like an epiphany or something."

Levin slumped on the couch after his monologue, his head drooping. Through the vacuum of her roaring Lucy suddenly felt what she later supposed could only have been compassion. She was no longer listening to the distant, abstract whimpering of children; this was a direct appeal. Her compassion was at once stronger and more demanding than the noise in her head, and she wanted to say something, anything. Her tongue clogged the words at first, stopped them in her throat. She tried again, opening her mouth slowly, as if it might stick. "Things will get better," she said, and the words came out unevenly, huskily, grating against one another like the gears on a rusted bicycle.

Levin raised his head, surprised but not completely startled. "You really talked, didn't you?" he asked.

Yes, she answered, yes, yes, her voice clearing and refining with each new word.

"I guess that had to happen eventually," he said, and he drew his long arms and legs in close to his body, folding up like a bridge chair.

The man she was involved with ten years later never knew about her childhood. It was not embarrassment or pain that kept Lucy from telling him; it just seemed fitting that she should be silent about her silence. Richard was a graduate student at the university, and Lucy was poet-in-residence for the semester. It bothered him that she was so reticent. His last lover, he said, was a full, loud, horsy woman. During lovemaking she would usually cry out, or chuckle low in her throat, or say, "Here. No, here." But Lucy was quiet, and she prided herself on it. "Sometimes," she wrote, "I even matched my breathing to his, so that when I was there, circling on the fine, quivering mercury of an orgasm, he would not hear a thing."

His old lover had accidentally left her hairbrush in the top dresser drawer when she moved out, and sometimes Lucy picked it up and examined it. It was a weighty mother-of-pearl affair with metal prongs. A good deal of the woman's hair was still woven around those prongs like string art, and Lucy imagined her standing before the mirror each evening, "brushing her coarse red hair with one hundred savage strokes, summoning up a fury of electricity."

Richard missed his old lover; Lucy could tell. One night she heard him speaking on the telephone in the kitchen, his voice low and conspiratorial. Lucy knew that he was talking to her.

She stayed up for a long time that night, thinking about Levin. She pictured the two of them meeting once again on the summer lawn of the hospital. "The grass would be heavy and wet with morning," she wrote, "and we would walk toward each other slowly, pulling two chairs out of the sun and into the vast, spreading shade of a cigarette tree."

chapter five

Claire liked to imagine that she was conceived amid gritty, damp sand and ice-cream wrappers on the shore of some anonymous beach at midnight. Her parents, mistakenly thinking themselves possessors of a new sort of freedom, most likely made love with abandon that night, unaware that behind every other dune, other couples were reveling in this very same, false phenomenon. The beach at midnight is nothing more than a series of open-air cubicles, a flea market for lovers who do not have much time or pride.

Claire's feelings about her parents worsened after Seth died. Two weeks after his death they decided the family needed to get away for a while, to be free of all the phone calls, the letters of condolence, the looks. They took Claire to Italy for a week. Claire remembered the vacation only in terms of speed. "Come on, we're late," her mother would say to her any time she lingered in a museum, and there would be a yank at her sleeve. They rushed her, relay-race fashion, from one end of the Sistine Chapel to the other. It was not the kind of vacation scene Claire had imagined, in which a young girl, bored within the confines of a museum, tugs at the fabric of her mother's dress. The mother stands casually before each painting and sculpture, ignoring the tugs, feeling very much at home.

But it would never be that way. Claire's parents pulled her, yanked her through her adolescence at breakneck speed. Museums were to be dashed through, dinners at restaurants to be choked down, clothes to be outgrown as quickly as possible and donated immediately to the Mt. Calvary people when they telephoned for contributions. "If you are coming at all, come now," her mother said over and over.

And now, home from college for Christmas five years later, things were no different. Nothing had slowed down at all. Claire walked out of the den, where her parents were arguing over whether or not they should renew their subscription to cable TV. She went into Seth's old room where everything was still in its proper place—the books, including *Danny Dunn and the Homework Machine*, which had been his childhood favorite, the oiled leather baseball glove, the slender glass bong way up on the top shelf. Claire sat down on the bed, where the clean sheets, she realized with a start, had probably not been changed in five years.

Her mother walked past, storming out of her fight. She saw Claire sitting in the room and poked her head in. "What are you doing in here?" she asked. Her face was pink, the way it was when she sat under the hair dryer for too long at the beauty parlor.

"I was just sitting here. Thinking. Is there something wrong with that?"

"No. But that's what you do all year at school. Isn't that why we send you to Swarthmore—so you can think? Now that you're home for a while, why don't you make yourself useful for a change? Come in and help me with dinner."

In the kitchen her mother talked rapidly, snapping green beans with each syllable. Claire dumped the snapped beans into a colander and ran cold water over them. Whenever she and her mother had a conversation, it was while doing some kind of busywork, preferably something that made a good deal of noise so that the gaps between their sentences could be gracefully filled.

"Well, Claire," her mother said. "What do you plan to do with this expensive education you're getting? Are you planning on doing nothing and going out to save the Indians, like your sister?"

Joan had stayed out in Arizona to live and work on a Walapai reservation. She saw the family once every few years, usually only for deaths or celebrations. Claire remembered her as being very tan and lean, her arms heavy with turquoise bracelets. When the two sisters embraced the last time Joan came East, Claire thought Joan smelled of the desert.

"I don't know what I plan on doing," Claire answered. "I'm only a sophomore. I have a little time to think about it."

"You sound just like your sister," her mother said. "She

always told me, 'Leave me alone, I have plenty of time, don't hassle me.' Then when she got out of school, she had no career plans at all. No skills, either. Nothing. You may major in English or whatever, Claire, but you're going to need something to fall back on." She began to scrape celery, the pale green threads flying into the garbage pail.

"Why are you so bitter?" Claire asked softly.

Her mother turned. "Bitter," she said after a moment. "You think I'm bitter? Wait until you turn fifty; you'll see that there's nothing to tap-dance about." She resumed her scraping.

Claire flicked on the blender, crushing some pineapple for dessert, and the kitchen became a battleground of noises. In a few minutes, with nothing left for either of them to do, there was quiet once again. "I'm sick of this," Claire said. "You're so nasty about everything. And Daddy is no better. He doesn't *do* anything; he just sits in the den all day."

"He has things on his mind," her mother said.

"I'm aware of that."

"A real smart-ass you turned out to be."

"Why aren't you ever nice to me?" Claire asked.

Her mother came close, waving the celery scraper in the air. "Look, Claire," she said, "I don't know what you want from me. You come home on vacation and give everybody a hard time. Things are difficult for all of us, you know. Why don't you try to accept things a little more? There's really nothing else we can do. Just stop questioning everything for a while, criticizing everything. We're all doing our best. Please, Claire, for me, okay? It gives me such a headache." As though to illustrate, she put down the scraper and lifted her hands to her head, forming a steeple that covered her eyes.

It was an awkward moment. Claire wondered if her mother was about to cry, if she should leave the room or possibly even apologize. But what would she apologize *for*?

In a second her mother dropped her hands, and her eyes were as clear and hard as ever. She had been nowhere near the point of tears. It seemed to Claire that all important confrontations between the two of them took place in the kitchen. She was reminded of something she had learned in high school Social Studies—about the high incidence of an army winning a war when it is fought on its own turf. Her mother was certainly the one in her element here, surrounded by gleaming copper and Formica, in the room where she had spent countless hours over the years.

Claire could not stay in the kitchen any longer. She went to the hall closet and put on her down jacket. "Where are you going?" her mother called as the front door closed.

It did not feel much better to be outside, although that was no surprise. Everything reminded her of childhood: the orange basketball hoop over the garage which was missing its net, and the hump in the driveway which she had stumbled over once, chipping a baby tooth. On the Danzigers' street, the split-level houses stood one after the other in rows a few yards back from the gutter, like attentive parade watchers.

Every evening the very last child on the block wheeled his bicycle home while it was still light, baseball cards flicking gently through the spokes, and the eight or so feet that separated the identical houses were just enough to keep sound insulated, just enough to keep family troubles within the family.

It began to do something—sleet, drizzle, hail, she couldn't tell which. She could feel wet chunks falling into her hair, and she made her way back home. Inside, dinner was already on the table, and her parents sat in their chairs, their forks poised in the air.

"We would have waited," her mother said, "but I had no idea of where you ran off to, and the food started to get cold. Sit down and join us. It's meat loaf."

It was as if nothing had happened. And really, Claire had to admit, nothing had.

Later that evening Julian called. "Hello," he said when she answered. "I miss you madly."

Claire unlooped the cord from where it was caught around a plastic plant and carried the phone halfway down the basement stairs. She liked to talk there; it was dark and silent. "I miss you too," she said.

"Have things been so terrible at your house?"

"Yes," she said. "They have."

"Oh," Julian said. 'I'm sorry to hear that."

"What have you been doing?" Claire asked.

"Reading, mostly. Just one book. Guess what it is."

"I have no idea."

"Just guess."

"I hate guessing games. If you're going to tell me, tell me."

"Okay," Julian said. "I was planning on waiting until we got back to school. I've been reading *Sleepwalking*." His voice was hushed. "You know, Claire, it's the most beautiful thing I've ever read. Lucy Ascher is really fine. You have good taste." He paused. "And besides, you taste good."

Claire did not laugh. He should know by now, she thought, that most things did not strike her as funny. Maybe that was the reason he said silly things to her, to try to change that. One night, during sex, he whispered, "You know something, Claire? There's a *vas deferens* between us." She had not even smiled, but he didn't seem to mind. It was as though he were keeping himself amused.

"Are you still there?" Julian asked on the phone. "Hello, Claire?"

"I'm still here," she answered. "I just don't know what you expect me to say or think. I mean, am I supposed to congratulate you for reading Lucy Ascher's book? Is it supposed to be some great feat?" Claire felt an obscure resentment. She wanted Lucy Ascher to herself. She did not want Julian snuggling up, trying to join in, as if it were a great game. Claire wanted to be the only one in the world who loved Lucy Ascher. She knew this was impossible and even silly, but she enjoyed pretending that she was Lucy Ascher's disciple, the only one in the world who felt such far-reaching sorrow and joy when thinking about her. A passion of that sort is not something you share with another person. It would create a threesome— an ungainly, cumbersome triangle. Claire suddenly felt protective, as though something were about to be taken from her.

This time it was Julian who did not say anything for a while, although she could hear him breathe. Through his mouth. "You know," he said at last, "I thought you would like it. I figured it would bring us closer together. I never know what's going on inside your mind, so I counted on the book helping me to understand a little better."

"Well," Claire said, "you were wrong. I'm sorry, you were just wrong. That's all there is to it." Then she hung up on him.

She had never done that to anyone and had always thought it very rude when she heard of other people doing it. She pictured Julian on the phone in his family's library, or whatever room he was in, somewhere deep inside his plush brownstone. There would be corking on the walls, she imagined, and the whole room would be done up in soft beiges and browns. He would be sitting on the edge of a deep corduroy couch, holding his touch-tone receiver a few inches from his ear, bewildered as he listened to the dead line.

Claire crouched on the stair in the darkness, holding herself tightly, and rocked back and forth. She had done this when she was very small, and it had always made her feel better. But now she suddenly became aware of how foolish it all was. She should calm herself down and call Julian back, ask his forgiveness and say she did not know what had come over her—it was just one of those things. But she did not want to. She wanted to stay in the basement forever, a kind of subterranean Mrs. Rochester.

"Oh, yes," her parents would say whenever they had company, "we have a daughter. She lives in the basement, and we have not seen her for a few years. We send her meals down on a pulley. Still, it's better than nothing, wouldn't you agree? Our two other children are no longer with us. Our son died and our elder daughter has gone off with the Indians. Claire is all we have."

Claire stood and walked upstairs, bumping the telephone over the steps behind her. Nothing made her happy except Lucy Ascher—that was what it all came down to. All of the squabbling with her parents and with Julian had no bearing on anything; she was just marking time. School meant nothing to her—she read all of the texts assigned and she diligently typed up her term papers, but she never paid close attention. She knew many college students felt a kind of apathy; she had overheard a couple of students having a conversation one day on the lunch line. One of them told the other that he was depressed, that he felt disinterested, alienated from the rest of the world, that he saw no point in going on with anything. His friend had smiled and told him in a sure voice that he was suffering from existentialism, the adolescent disease.

All around her, people complained of having a void within them that could not be filled. The difference between her and them was that she *had* something to fill her void. The only problem was that she did not have enough time in which to do it. There was course work to contend with, and Julian, and her family. Her head buzzed with trivial chores and responsibilities.

She did not speak to Julian for the remainder of the vacation. She refused to phone, and she knew that he had too much pride to call her again. She spent almost all of her time in her bedroom, reading Lucy Ascher's poetry, slowly regressing into the routine she had followed in high school. Each evening she selected a poem to be read first thing in the morning. She slept fitfully; her nights were filled with broken-up, puzzling dreams that made her call out in her sleep. She woke very early, with the birds screaming outside, and read poetry in the dim light of her room. Her parents ignored her.

She went back to Swarthmore on a Sunday, arriving in the evening. The campus was covered with snow and looked quite beautiful. Everything was still; many students had not yet returned. Claire dropped her orange valise in her room and walked across the green. The snow was up to her shins, but she liked the feel of coldness seeping in over the tops of her boots. She knocked on the door of Naomi's room. She had not been there in a long while, and she wanted to talk to her.

"Come in," Naomi called. She and Laura were sitting on the floor, drinking tea they had brewed in an illegal hot pot.

"Well, hello," Laura said. "Fancy seeing you here." Her voice was cool.

"I'm in bad shape," Claire said from the doorway. "I need you two."

"You need *us*?" Laura asked. "After snubbing us for half a semester, you suddenly need us? I can't tell you how flattered I am."

"Come on," said Naomi before Laura could add anything more. "Leave her alone. What's the matter, Claire? Is something really wrong?"

Claire came in and sat down on the floor between them. She had spent many nights sitting in that very same spot, and the wood felt comforting now, familiar. "I just can't get by anymore," she said. "I've completely fucked up everything between Julian and me. I can't stand the idea of going to classes, or writing papers, or sleeping with Julian, or anything. It's all a nightmare to me. I hated being home, and I hated coming back to school."

"Do you know what's causing it?" Naomi asked, pouring her a mug of tea.

"I think so," Claire answered. "I mean, I know so." She told them about how she had discovered that Lucy was the only thing that mattered in her life. When she finished speaking, the three of them sat and drank their tea in silence.

"You know," Naomi said finally, "we're all pretty obsessed with our poets. Most people think it's pretty sick. But you have to forget all that. You just have to go with your instincts, Claire."

"What do you mean?"

Naomi said in a quiet voice, "I went through a similar time last summer. I was really unhappy and out of things. I didn't know what to do with myself. I was working as a waitress at that awful resort on the Cape; you know all that. Anyway, I was wrapped up in Sylvia that summer, just like I am now, but it sort of incapacitated me then. I used to drop trays and daydream and take long walks by myself down the beach. This is going to sound really stupid, but one day I was serving these two men their drinks, and one of them said to the other, 'Well, Phil, here's a hair of the dog that bit you,' and they both laughed and downed their drinks."

"I don't understand," Claire said. "What's the point?"

"I haven't gotten to that yet," Naomi said. "I realized right then that what *I* needed was a hair of the dog. I mean, in order to be cured of Sylvia, at least to the point where I could think about other things occasionally, I had to immerse myself a little more in her. I had to take a risk."

On her day off, she had borrowed a car from one of the other waitresses and driven to Wellesley, the town in which Sylvia Plath grew up and where her mother still lived. She parked the car in downtown Wellesley and walked to the block where Plath's house was. She sat down under a tree directly across the street and waited for something to happen. She watched the house all morning—an old white frame house with a neatly trimmed front lawn. After an hour had gone by, the door opened, and an elderly woman walked out. She got into the car that was parked in the driveway and drove off. Naomi recognized her at once as Aurelia Plath, mother of Sylvia. She sat unmoving under the tree and waited for another hour. The car drove back up, and Aurelia stepped out, her arms laden with grocery bags. She fumbled with a key ring and let herself into the house, closing the door behind her. She had not noticed Naomi. That was all that had taken place. But it had been enough—that little, tantalizing slice of Plath life, the wisp of a white curtain that showed through the living-room window, the dark, hazy shapes inside that were pieces of furniture. Naomi stepped out from her place under the branches and drove back to the Cape, satisfied.

"I don't know," Claire said. "I don't think I could ever do anything like that—spying, I mean. I would feel very sneaky."

"But is it enough for you just to read Ascher's books? Does that make you happy enough?" Naomi asked.

Claire thought about this. "No," she said slowly, "I guess it doesn't."

The tea was getting colder. Claire wrapped her hands around the mug, capturing the last bit of its warmth.

"I think you should go there." Claire was startled—it was Laura speaking, angry Laura, who had not said anything for nearly an hour. "I did a similar thing," she admitted. "I went to see Anne Sexton's grave. I spent the afternoon at the cemetery, kneeling in the grass in front of the gravestone. I know they say you're not supposed to do that, because it's like stepping on the person herself. Somehow, that thought appealed to me. Not stepping on her, just being with her. I knelt on the grass, and I felt I was really there, with Anne, on a typical day of her life. It was as if we were two good friends having a casual conversation. I talked to her about a lot of things—her poetry, of course, and her marriage, and then we got around to the subject of death. I even cried a little. She wanted: 'Rats Live on No Evil Star' put on her headstone. That's a palindrome, a phrase that reads the same backward and forward, that she saw painted on the side of a barn somewhere and always loved. She said she wanted it to be her epitaph. I put flowers there when I left that afternoon—a big bunch of peonies."

Claire did not know what to think. It was getting late now. She should either go home or stay for a marathon evening. What was it, she wondered, that attracted the three of them to their poets? Why not pick a living, happy poet whom you could write to and maybe even hope to meet someday? The fact that all three of the poets were suicides made it even worse;

when Claire thought of Lucy Ascher in her last hours, she wanted to cry. She wanted to swoop down and pull Lucy off that bridge.

"Were you planning on having a meeting tonight?" she asked timidly. "If you don't want me to come, I'll understand and all."

Naomi smiled. "What do you think we're doing right now?" she asked. "What do you think all this talk is?"

It was true. They were all sitting in a huddled little group, a troika, speaking their innermost thoughts about their poets. "In that case," Claire said, "I'm glad to be back."

Laura slid in closer, and the circle tightened. Naomi lit a hand-dipped candle, shut off the lights, and the scent of bayberry rose and filled the room. It was just like old times.

Part 2

chapter six

In the early morning Lucy bent and ran her hand under the bathtub faucet, checking to see if it was warm enough. Warm enough for what, though? She was not altogether sure. You were supposed to run water into a bathtub when you slit your wrists; that was all she knew. She was not sure if it coaxed the blood, or if it just made you more at ease and let you fold first into sleep, then death.

The bathroom seemed especially bright that morning. "There was nothing anywhere that gave evidence of human usage," she later wrote in her journal, "with the exception of a single long, blond hair delicately snaking across a tile on the wall." She turned off the tap and stepped into the shallow water. It was quite hot, and vapor lifted up from around her ankles. She felt self-conscious, posed as she stood naked, like

Botticelli's Venus. Lucy had taken off her terrycloth bathrobe and now it lay in a soft, sad bundle in the corner. She sat down on the very edge of the tub and picked up the razor she had placed there. So this was really it.

She had known that the summer would end like this for her, that things could not keep going the way they had been. She had slipped out of the rhythm of the city, had awakened one morning and felt overwhelmed by the prospect of even getting out of bed. She forced herself to stand; it was too humid to lie there, and the room was too close. "The air was thick with its heat, and with my own," she wrote. "Summer is a time when everything rubs against everything else. People seem to grate against each other when they touch, when they make love. The friction is too high, and I am losing my endurance."

She touched the razor lightly to her wrist, like a wand, and a stripe of blood appeared. "There was hardly any pain," she wrote, "not even the slight shiver and rush that accompanies a paper cut. I did my other wrist then, in the same way. I kept thinking of heat, of hopelessness. I looked downward and felt only surprise at seeing my own blood, nothing more."

From down the hall there were sounds of people waking up. It was the heart of August, and Lucy was living in a tiny room in a Barnard dormitory. There were fifteen other students staying there for the summer, but she was friends with none of them. She fixed her dinners on a hot plate: cans of soup or Spaghettios. She worked as a waitress afternoons, and from carrying trays loaded down with dishes her arms had become muscular. They looked useless to her now, though, as she sat on the smooth tub edge. Blood left her quickly.

"I felt a quiver in my eyelid, a tic of fatigue in the midst of everything. I wanted to leave the hot bathroom. I thought about a play I had once seen in which Limbo is depicted as a large steambath, and I wondered if I was letting myself be sucked into Limbo, if I was fated to remain in the confines of the damp, airless bathroom for eternity. All my life I have felt closed off from everything—living behind a film of mist, and now I wondered if it was the same thing, even in death."

Lucy stood up, as wobbly as the time she had given blood to the Red Cross. She slipped into her yellow bathrobe and left the room. Lines of blood forked down her wrists—she could even cup some in her hands. She felt truly faint now, and the lights dimmed, brightened, then dimmed again, as if an intermission had ended and the second act of a show were about to begin. Summoned, she made the few yards back down the hall. She fell onto her narrow bed and dialed University Health Services. She was sitting there, eyes closed, leaning against the headboard, when they came for her a few minutes later.

"My dark hair spread out on the pillow of the stretcher. This was pure softness now—the pale-green blanket they placed over me, the gentle way they tucked in the loose edges. The sharp sound of adhesive tape being pulled from a roll brought me up to the surface. As they wrapped my left wrist, then my right, I knew I would live, but somehow that knowledge was irrelevant. I was not even sure of why I had done it in the first place. It seemed just another action, another piece of business to fill a long day. I gravitate toward death, toward any kind of promise of a release from consciousness. I had an early memory then that sprang from nowhere. I saw myself as a pink, creased infant lying in a bassinet, with a big face loom-ing over me. My mother, maybe? My father?

"Once my mother said, 'We will always be here for you, Lucy,' and I guess she meant it. That was the summer I stopped talking, though, and I knew that no one was really there for me, that I was on my own. The faces of my parents sometimes blend into one image—a kindly, ambiguous guardian face that can be seen from every angle, like the moon from a car window as you drive home at night. But unlike the moon, the face is there even when I close my eyes. It's just out of grasp, and I find myself alone, as always.

"I have sometimes felt like an orphan. Once in a depart-ment store I became separated from my parents. A saleswoman approached me and asked if I had lost my mother. 'I have no parents,' I told her and watched as her face slowly changed. The words had spilled from me naturally, as though I were used to saying them, as though they were really true.

"It wasn't that my mother and father did not love me, or don't love me even now; they do in their own resigned, puzzled way. I was constantly aware of being separate from them, a foster child in an inappropriate home. I had figured out early that things would remain this way. There was nothing I could do, nothing I could touch. My childhood had no gravity. I floated dumbly through it, reaching out to grab for doorknobs, bedposts. I could not grab for people, because early on I would watch my father's face, his lips moving slightly as he read the print of a huge marine biology text, and I could see that he was doing all he could just to *be*, and that nobody can really do any better. Until there is no longer the possibility of sadness, of isolation, there can be no gravity. We all float by, rootless, taking clumsy astronaut steps and calling it progress.

"My mother came to me in the hospital, clutching her red pocketbook and looking so out of place, so lost. She came and stood at the foot of my bed, just watching me. Someone cried across the big room; this was an adult cry, unlike the sounds of children I used to hear at night during that summer so long ago. A nurse whispered to my mother that I was stabilized, and this seemed so ironic that I smiled. I didn't think I would ever be really stabilized. I had been given a sedative, and could feel its dull glaze start to move evenly over me. My mouth was loose and dry. I had nothing to say to my mother, and I hoped she would leave soon, go back to the beach, the only place she seemed to fit. Everything is grainy there, like the texture of a blown-up photograph. The ground is broken up into an uneven surface, like a page of Braille. Everywhere you walk there are tiny surprises—shell chips with their color bleached away, ridged Coca-Cola caps, the empty husks of men-of-war. Some- how my mother and father feel at home there.

"We used to dig for China. My whole family would burrow in the sand until we reached the depth where it became dark and wet, not like sand at all, and we could not dig any farther. That was my favorite part—the core of the beach—all of the graininess gone. Your fingers touch clay, touch a new, smooth plane. I imag- ined an underground world, a country where the inhabitants knew the beauty of the darkness, and weren't afraid of it.

" 'Is this China?' I would ask my parents. 'Have we reached China yet?'

" 'Almost,' they would answer. 'Almost.'"

———

Helen's skin had many acids in it, and every time she wore a silver or gold chain, she wound up with a fine black band of tarnish on her neck. According to her husband, this was a sure indication of royalty in the blood. She had always viewed it in a different way. When she observed herself in the wavy-glassed mirror above the sink, the band appeared more as a dissecting line, etched in a perfect semicircle directly above her collarbone. Cut on dotted line.

She thought abstractly of supermarket coupons. Lately she had been collecting these fragments of paper, shredding them from glossy magazines whenever she found them, even in the doctor's waiting room while the receptionist's hawk eye was focused elsewhere. It was not the redemption of these money savers that intrigued her, but the actual collection itself. She hoarded them, the way her husband, Ray, collected bivalve mollusk shells. Feverishly, as though on a scavenger hunt. It filled the hours; it was better than nothing. "Just so I don't have to think," Helen had said to a friend once. "That's all I ask for."

It was winter in Southampton, and the ocean was choppy and looked darker than ever. Helen was stewing tomatoes and onions in the kitchen while Ray read an oceanography journal.

"Do you want to drive into East Hampton to a movie tonight?" he asked. "They're showing *Kramer vs. Kramer*."

"I don't care," she said. "Whatever you want. You know that none of that matters to me."

Ray sighed and closed the magazine. He placed his hands

flat on the kitchen table. "There's nothing I can do to make you feel any better, is there?" he asked.

She did not answer him.

"Maybe you should go back to see Len Deering. He would put you on those antidepressants again if you asked. They seemed to help you last time."

"They just masked things," Helen said, "and they made me fat. I couldn't fit into any of my clothes, and I just sat and cried all day. Remember? Nothing can really help."

Ray stood up and put his arms around her. He did this at least once a day, as though to remind her that he was still there, still concerned, still grieving along with her.

They went to the movie after dinner, driving in silence. Ray put on the radio, and static came in. There were no really good stations this far out on the island. Snow was starting to fall again. It had been snowing sporadically all evening, stopping every hour or so as if for a breath. Helen used to think it always looked so beautiful when it snowed on the ocean. The flakes landed and settled themselves for a moment, before disappearing under the surface.

As they walked down the aisle of the theater, scanning the rows for two vacant seats near the front, a few people watched them, then looked discreetly away. Helen pretended not to notice. She held on to Ray's arm and they kept walking. During the movie he leaned over and whispered into her ear, "How long can we continue like this?" It was not a new question. He asked it periodically and she always replied, "Until we drop dead." He squeezed her hand hard. Their running dialogue had become a sort of private joke between them.

Friends used to tell Helen that eventually she would start to feel better, that one day out of the blue she would wake up and begin her morning without thinking of her daughter. She believed this for a while—clung to it, in fact. One day, she thought, she would indeed get up and feel refreshed from her sleep. She would start teaching again. She would set up the badminton net on the beach and they would play for hours. She'd cook jelly omelettes for herself and for Ray, and they would both sit at the table and discuss the lectures they would be giving in their sections that day.

When one year had passed, Helen knew this would not happen. She felt no better. There had been no major change. Friends ceased to be so optimistic about her state. They telephoned less often; they couldn't bear to hear her cry anymore. There was something almost unnatural about overly long mourning periods, something almost indecent.

Helen turned her leave from teaching into an early retirement. She stayed at home each day, sitting out on the back porch overlooking the water.

"You shouldn't let your child become the focus of your life," a psychologist had told her and Ray many years earlier. This had seemed like unrealistic advice. What did he know? He was not even married, this expert. He knew nothing about what it meant to have a child.

Some people had it easy. Some people could just drop off their child at an expensive summer camp in the Poconos and then knock around Europe by themselves until the close of the season. When they returned they could simply retrieve their daughter, who would be bronzed and happy and voted Best in Dodgeball.

Not so with Helen and Ray Ascher. They had spent their time worrying and consulting professionals. Lucy had always seemed a space apart, locked in some very private world. She was overly sensitive when she was little; if you sneaked up behind her and tickled her, she jumped and turned very pale and could not be consoled for hours.

"Where did we ever get her?" Helen used to say when Lucy was a child. It was as though Lucy had fallen from a star, so different was she. And then, when she was twelve, she had simply stopped talking for two months. They had never understood what went on inside her. In junior high school Lucy began to write poetry—complicated, elegiac things that neither Helen nor Ray could really grasp. The child of two marine biologists, two lower-power academics—two serious, practical people out on the windy tip of Long Island—was a poet. Go figure that out, Helen thought.

"You're a *poet* and you don't *know it*," Ray used to say to Lucy, chucking her under the chin.

They never knew what she thought of them. Did she think them simple, unartistic? When she received an award from the New York State Council on the Arts, she had thanked them in her speech. Helen and Ray had sat in the front row of the auditorium, bewildered and proud. Helen's pumps had felt tight and all wrong. She had been wearing sandals for years now on the beach and loafers in the classroom.

Sometimes crazy thoughts went through Helen's head. Maybe Lucy was put on this earth for some divine purpose. Maybe she and Ray were not Lucy's true parents, maybe they were just the facilitators of her birth—she the mortar and he the pestle, as it were, grinding up and preparing the ingredients of this spectacular creation.

After Lucy killed herself, Helen found that she often thought about Lucy's conception for some reason, trying to remember it in minute detail. She didn't know why she had latched on to this, but she could not stop thinking about it. Lucy was conceived while Helen and Ray were spending a weekend in Southampton. His Aunt Mary had died and left Ray's family her summer house. "You kids might as well use it," Ray's father said. "You're young, enjoy it."

They drove out to the beach every Friday and stayed until very late Sunday night. They almost couldn't bear to go back to Brooklyn. "This is where we really belong," Ray said, and he was right. Later, when Southampton College opened, they both got faculty positions, and Helen made the move from the city to the beach with ease.

But it was those early days, when the house was theirs only during the weekend, that Helen remembered most clearly. One Saturday in 1954, as Ray was about to leave the house and spend the day exploring the area, Helen stopped him in the hallway. "Wait," she said shyly. "Would you like to go back to bed for a little while?"

Ray stopped and put down the bag lunch she had packed him: a sandwich without the crusts, cut into neat triangles, a nectarine carefully checked for scars and soft spots, and a thermos of coffee, black as pitch. They did not go into the bedroom but made love right on the warped wooden floor of the hallway. The salt air had made the whole house buckle.

Ray smiled over and then under her, smiled as she moved her hips to his. Just as in formal dancing, here she would never take the lead. She would never initiate a rhythm; she always left it up to him. This control seemed to frighten Ray, but somehow this fear must have been arousing. He placed his hands on her bottom, and pulled her up to him frantically. It was an action that might be taken by a person waking up to a house full of fire—a survival action, pulling a lover or child smack against his body as they wove their way through a thicket of flames.

Helen had wanted very much to conceive. They had been trying for months, and after they made love that morning, she lay flat on her back on the floor, her hands on her stomach. "Oh," she said suddenly.

"What is it?" Ray asked in a worried voice.

"I just felt something," she told him. "Inside me, moving around. Like the beginnings of a baby, I think."

He laughed at her. "That's ridiculous."

"No," she insisted, "I think this time it really worked. I actually *feel* pregnant." An image flitted through her mind: a microscopic fetus, its proportions minnowlike, almost all head and eyes, sucking its thumb somewhere deep inside of her. Ray laid his head down on his wife's stomach, listening closely for signs of life.

Are you ever happy?" Helen had asked her daugher once, when Lucy was eighteen.

"What do *you* think?" Lucy answered. Helen never brought the subject up again.

Lucy's poetry matured early—long, graceful poems that were accepted by small literary magazines. She went off to Barnard, but she did not get much out of it, and she dropped out after three semesters. "The education's too narrow," she said. Helen did not know what that meant. She only knew that Lucy was a rarity, and that she needed to be left alone. Sometimes, though, she had to be fished up by her parents.

She had first tried to kill herself when she was eighteen, spending the summer living in a hot Barnard dormitory, working as a waitress in a Beef 'n Brew by day and writing poems long into the night. Something had come unstuck, and Helen received a phone call from a doctor at Columbia Presbyterian, telling her that Lucy had slit her wrists and was in the hospital.

Ray was out on a sea expedition that day, and Helen took the train into the city by herself, feeling as if she might faint at any moment. At the hospital Lucy's room was large—a ward, really, with freshly made beds, hospital corners tucked in meticulously.

Lucy was over by the window, lying flat on her back. Helen came and stood by the foot of the bed, unable to think of anything right to say. She had trouble collecting her thoughts at all. She just shook her head slowly and said, "Lucy."

Lucy did not say anything but sighed heavily and moved a stray strand of hair from her eyes. Helen looked around the room helplessly. The woman in the next bed was watching the scene with rude interest. She leaned her head on her hands and stared very closely. She was a round-bodied woman with an equally round face. Helen turned away and knew that she was going to cry. She dug in her purse for a tissue and wept silently into it for a while.

"What's she crying for?" the woman asked anyone who would listen. "She thinks she's so special. What's she crying for?"

"Listen, I have to go," Helen said to Lucy all of a sudden. "God, I'm sorry, but I have to go. I'll be back tomorrow, with Dad. We can talk then." She leaned over to kiss Lucy, then she left. She walked out slowly, looking at all of the women in their beds. Lucy was by far the youngest; she was a child, really.

Television sets flickered soundlessly, showing anonymous women winning prizes on game shows, screaming their hearts out and yet not making a noise. The women in the ward looked doped-up and tired, as if they were just now coming to the surface after anesthesia. In this room, where nurses paced the floor like night watchmen in the bleak hours, lay fragmented women. They were women who did not resist the jab of a needle that would send them into a false sleep. At eighteen, Lucy was one of them.

It felt good to leave the hospital. I am a terrible mother, Helen thought. I have walked right out of there, just glided out the door. I didn't even ask her why or how or any of the vital questions. I didn't even sit there and just hold her hand.

Helen got on the subway, and with an extra bit of bravado sat down next to a man of questionable character. He was absently fingering his fly, as if it were a banjo and he were plucking out some rambling, distant tune.

She was able to get in touch with Ray later that day. The

Coast Guard radioed him in, said it was an emergency. She met him at the dock, and he fell into her arms, still wearing half a wet suit. "What is it?" he asked. "What is it?" She told him and she hugged him hard, until they both smelled of brine and kelp.

Years later they were plagued by people—writers, lonelies, crazies. Helen had the phone number changed and their listing plucked from the directory when Lucy died, but even so, people got through, as if by sheer will alone. They called late at night mostly, when their need was at its strongest. "Hello?" they usually whispered or shrieked, asking it like a question, not believing they had connected. "Are you the mother of Lucy Ascher?"

They would swallow down their sobs and tell how much they loved Lucy's work and ask how Helen and Ray went on with their day-to-day existence. What had Lucy actually been like? they asked with urgency. Had Helen and Ray gotten over it yet? Would they ever?

There was a journalist sent on assignment from a slick news magazine who, when the interview ended, hung around, clearly not wanting to leave. This was just after the publication of *Sleepwalking*, and Helen and Ray sat on the couch stiffly while the woman toyed with her pad and pencil and the light meter on her Pentax for too long a time.

"Well," Helen said, exhaling a soft whoosh of air, trying to finalize things.

The journalist looked up from her camera, eyes suddenly desperate. "I can't tell you," she said, "how much this has meant to me. I've been begging my department head for this article for weeks." She touched Helen's and Ray's hands, as if performing a benediction. "Thank you," she said, "for spawning Lucy Ascher."

Spawning. Wasn't that word usually associated with fish—mother guppies spawning hundreds of little translucent babies, only to eat most of them minutes after birth. In a moment of cockeyed philosophy Helen thought, Maybe we all eat our children. When they are born we press them to ourselves with an air of propriety, searching their faces for shared features, thrilled when we think we see a familiar cast to the eyes. Your nose. My mouth. The baby is born with a set of hand-me-downs.

Helen stood up and said to the woman, "I think you'd better go." Realizing how this must sound, she added, "It's supposed to rain, and these roads can get pretty bad."

After the woman left, Ray and Helen stood facing each other in the living room. Ray had been a wrestler in college, and his shoulders and chest, though long unworked, still made him look hulking. He was big all over, and he had trouble pulling sweaters over his head. She had to help him sometimes as he fumbled like a large, unformed animal trying to slip into a more finished skin.

Now his largeness filled the living room and she felt sorry for him, for them both. Not exactly sorry, more embarrassed as they loomed over the furniture in their living room, helpless in their house by the water.

It would be naïve to have been completely surprised by Lucy's death, to choke into a reporter's thrust-out microphone, "My God, we had no idea, no idea at all." There wasn't anything that particularly surprised Helen. She understood none of it, and never had. When Lucy was hospitalized for not speaking at the age of twelve, her doctor had said to Helen and Ray, "You are going to have your hands full with your child."

Helen had not agreed with this statement. She took all things literally. Maybe, she was to think years later, that was why she had no ear for poetry. We are not going to have our hands full with Lucy, she knew; we are going to have them empty. Lucy never permitted real touching of any kind. If Helen reached out to stroke down the fine dark hair of her daughter, Lucy ducked away like a hand-shy dog. "Mo-om," she would say, annoyed, "cut it *out*." Lucy allowed her no closeness, nothing to hold on to. When she was little they took her out on the boat every Sunday, but she had no makings of a good sailor. She steered rigidly, not letting the boat ride with the wind, always fighting a natural current.

They took her to the marine biology laboratory at the college and let her look at plankton under a powerful microscope. She spent an hour peering at different slides, and Helen and Ray sat together at the other end of the long, narrow room, happy that they had gotten through to her. Finally Lucy rose and walked over to them. There was a faint half-moon under her eye from pressing it to the ocular. "Well," said Helen, "you seemed to be really enjoying yourself. I'm glad."

"It was boring," Lucy said. "Can we go home now?"

So their arms were empty with her, a paradox that seemed to contain the stuff of a Zen koan: When can one's arms be both full and empty? The solution, after years of traveling the road to higher consciousness, comes easily: when they are embracing Lucy Ascher.

Yes, Helen thought, we spawned her, that is all.

There were various signs along the way that clearly showed something was out of kilter. One night when Lucy was sixteen, Helen was wakened out of a thick sleep by the strains of the national anthem. In the dead-serious logic applied by dreamers and people in the throes of delirium, Helen figured that she must be a truly patriotic person at heart—the kind of person who dreams the whole of the national anthem, a version complete with woodwinds, percussion, brass, strings, and even the sporadic *ping* of a triangle asserting its delicate presence.

Helen blinked herself fully awake and realized she had not been dreaming. Ray slept next to her on his stomach, the blanket a tent over his head. Helen stepped into her green slippers and padded into the living room, from where the music seemed to come. There she saw Lucy sitting on the couch, the national anthem blaring from the television set. The music stopped abruptly, and an announcer said in a wilting voice, "This is WNEW, Channel Five, ending our programing day."

"Lucy?" Helen asked.

Lucy gasped, turning. "Oh, you surprised me, Mom," she said.

"I heard the music and thought it was a dream," said Helen. "What are you doing up at this hour?"

"I couldn't sleep. I never can," Lucy answered. She turned her face to the ceiling and stretched her arms out at her sides.

It was there, in that early-morning confrontation, that Helen took in the completeness of the pain that her daughter held out to her, palms up, like an offering. Helen did not know from where the pain sprang, and she could not even begin to guess its source. She saw it the way a tourist might see an impressive landmark geyser—focusing only on the arrow-beam of water spouting upward, never thinking about its origin, that hot, dark lake that must lie like the Styx underground. It was that simple vision that stayed with Helen long after.

She came and sat down on the couch next to Lucy. "Are you all right?" she asked. "I never can tell whether you're very unhappy or just overly serious for a sixteen-year-old."

In the early days of Helen's relationship with Ray (their courtship, they used to call it, snickering), Helen often thought he was very depressed. When she questioned him, he seemed shocked. "I'm not in the least depressed," he said. "I'm just thinking."

Both of their families lived in Brooklyn then, but it was on the beach in Rockaway in 1941 that they first met. Ray was a freshman at City College, and he told her that he had convinced his parents to let the family go to the beach for the vacation rather than to the same small kosher hotel in the Catskills where they had gone for the past ten years. Ray had taken an oceanography course that spring semester and had fallen in love with oceans—with the idea of them, at least.

They met right in front of the water where he was looking in the sand for interesting shells and she was sunning herself with a three-sided aluminum foil reflector. Ray loomed over her and peered down. Her eyes were closed, of course, so he coughed lightly to attract her attention. She opened her eyes and saw the crinkled reflection of a boy in the foil. He was big and pale—had obviously not been in the sun much.

"God, you're tan," he said, and it was true. Although her family had been at the beach for only two days, she and her sister had been sunning themselves on the blacktop roof of their apartment building in Bensonhurst for two weeks, and Helen knew she looked good. She was wearing her white bathing suit with the vertical stripes, a choice that would, the salesgirl had assured her, show off both her tan and her svelte figure.

Ray was pale but muscular—a combination, she quickly assessed, of the pensive student and the good athlete. Some indoor sport, probably. He brought his shell collection over to her chair and knelt in the warm sand alongside her, explaining things and letting her look through his pocket shell-identification handbook.

"See," he said, pointing to a color illustration, "this is the wedding cake Venus, really called *Callanatis disjecta*. You can only find it in Australian waters. I'd like to go there someday. And this is the lion's paw, the *Lyropectan nodosus*. This one's easier; you only have to go down to Florida to find it."

She and Ray were wearing different suntan lotions that day, she noticed. Hers was a sweet coconut oil for skin that tanned easily, his was a medicinal lotion for people who burned. It seemed to Helen that these smells were distinctly male and female—counterparts, almost. The bitter and the sweet. He leaned across to point out an illustration of a conch he especially liked, and their shoulders made accidental contact. They skidded against each other from the grease, and both laughed nervously. That gliding—she thought of it months later in bed with Ray, when he parted her legs and then moved between them as if by accident, as if he were performing some mindless act. They had laughed nervously then, too, surprised at feeling no friction.

Their families lived in adjacent pastel bungalows that summer. They were tiny, cheaply constructed houses with rooms that tumbled into one another. The vertical and horizontal frame parts around the windows and doors met unevenly, like the back seams of a man's poorly sewn suit jacket. Still, each house offered an ocean view—a small square window in the kitchen that opened out onto the beach.

Helen's mother stayed in there most of the day, not doing any genuine cooking but listening to her favorite radio programs and fixing box lunches for her husband and daughters to eat on the beach. She kept an electric fan on at all times, but all it did was whip up the old bungalow air that smelled of previous tenants. One especially muggy afternoon Helen's father came into the house, scooped her up in his arms and carried her outside. "You're going to get some sun on your face, Bella," he said in a loud voice. Everyone on the beach looked up from their foil reflectors for a second. "And you're going to get some sand between your toes." She laughed and gave in without resistance, but the very next morning she was back in the kitchen. She never went out on the beach again.

Helen knew her mother could see her from her post at the kitchen window, so she and Ray were discreet on the beach throughout the summer. They mostly talked, ate Eskimo pies, examined seaweed and shells, and swam. Once she rubbed lotion in expanding circles onto his back, and once he kept his hand flat on her thigh under a towel. They would wait until they got back to Brooklyn.

It was Ray who convinced her to go to Hunter College. She majored in biology because of him, and her greatest joy was when they studied together in the evenings. They planned to be famous marine biologists, a husband-and-wife team, and write a book together like Rachel Carson's *Under the Sea Wind*. They planned to live on the beach all year round someday.

Ray came and picked her up at night at her family's apartment. If she was not quite ready, she would send her little sister Miriam down to tell him to wait, and would watch from the window. Ray did not like sitting in the apartment with her parents, so he would stand under the streetlight at the corner, his head tucked into his broad chest, his hat tilted low on his head like a gangster's, smoking a Lucky Strike.

They were married in April of her freshman year at Hunter. He was a junior at CCNY then, and they moved into a basement apartment in her parents' building. Her mother was close friends with the landlord's wife and was able to get them a very good price. It was amazing, Helen thought, how different life was without sunlight. Ray worked in an office after classes and would come home in the evening, and they would make love on the fold-out bed. Even with the lights on, things were dim. They liked to look at each other. Before they were married they made love until their bodies were streamlined with sweat, under the trees in Prospect Park. It was the most daring thing Helen had ever done in her life. The second most daring thing (which actually didn't count, Ray claimed, because it was related) was going to her cousin Felice's gynecologist for a contraceptive. Felice, a senior at Hunter, had admittedly been having sex for years.

So Helen came home on the subway with a diaphragm nestled deep in her purse. That night, in the darkness of the copse of trees, the diaphragm glowed on the grass. Dusty with cornstarch, it looked otherworldly—a miniature spaceship that had just gently landed. She ran her hand along the side of Ray's body. Dark-brown hair fanned out in a funnel shape up from his navel and across his broad chest. This was it—the sound of her own zipper being undone along the back of her dress gave her a strange, wonderful feeling like the tug of a parachute's rip cord, possibly one that has been packed wrong, so that during the descent no cloth comes mushrooming out. Like most things, there was always that chance. Helen let herself drop.

She had been cleaning out Lucy's room—someone had to do it—when she found the notebook. Way at the bottom of her underwear drawer beneath a neat white pile of clothes which Lucy had folded as meticulously as a flag at sundown. A plain, blue, three-section spiral notebook. Lucy had been dead a week and a half, and Helen went through her things with care. She considered getting rid of the book, unread, but changed her mind. When a person dies, Helen thought, she leaves her secrets to the world as a kind of legacy.

Helen had a great-aunt who left the family the confidential recipe for her dish, "Minnie's Lighter-Than-Air Egg Kichel," when she died. As far as Helen knew, none of the relatives had yet remembered to try it out. So much for secrets. Helen opened the notebook at once. On the inside of the front cover Lucy had penned: "These are notes to myself, so I will never, never lose anything in the clutter of growing older."

The handwriting was tiny and difficult to read. Every line of every page was filled with it. Ray came into the room while Helen was reading. She heard him and glanced up. "Look," she said softly. It was as if she were pointing out an exotic bird or small animal that had found its way onto the porch, her voice low so as not to frighten it off. Ray came and sat Indian style beside her, and they read their daughter's notebook together.

It did not change anything. When they closed the book three hours later, they looked at each other, unsure. "I understand that she was in pain," Helen said, "but I don't understand why. I never will."

"Maybe we can't because we're too close to it all," Ray offered. "Maybe we need some objectivity."

The next morning Helen and Ray took the train into New York. It was the first day they had been outside in over a week. Were all noises somehow louder? They had been sitting in the still cocoon of their house for nine days, with people moving quietly in and out of the front door every few hours. Now Helen and Ray rode the subway up to Lucy's agent's office, unannounced. They had come to this decision the night before.

Vivian greeted them with quiet surprise. She had been out to the house the previous week, and they had not mentioned anything to her about coming to the office. She took their hands in her own firm grip. "Come in," she said. "I've just been doing some boring paperwork."

Her office was sunny and small. Helen and Ray sat and drank coffee. "How can I help you?" Vivian asked at last, leaning across the glass desktop.

They told her, their voices interrupting each other, chiming in, amending things, about the notebook. Helen drew it from her purse and handed it across the desk. "We thought this should be looked at, and maybe something should be done with it," she said.

In a little less than a year, *Sleepwalking* was published. The book evoked a strong current of sorrow and attention, and the Aschers received letters each morning, phone calls each night. This was the way things would go on until the end, it seemed. At the funeral, when Len Deering, friend and psychiatrist, had leaned over and gently asked if Helen "wanted anything," she quickly nodded. She took the Elavil faithfully each day, letting herself blur into passivity. It was a change of pace, anyway.

On the beach, that constant white strip, there was also a change. Vacationers left the area to go back to their other lives; the summer had ended. The air cooled and the water followed. Helen and Ray dragged in the chaise longues from their back porch, scraping them across the redwood planks, and put up the storm windows. They worked together in the house, side by side. They made love occasionally, even though Helen felt no real pull of sexual feeling.

People came and went quietly, on the balls of their feet, it seemed, in a continuation of the condolence ritual of constant guests. The theory was loosely that the mourning family should never be left alone. Friends from the marine biology department came and sat on the edge of their chairs, drumming out small rhythms on the living-room table. They drank the Earl Grey tea that Helen brewed, and the cup would rock in its saucer. No one knew what to do in the presence of such untapped grief. A silent hysteria hovered over the beach house like a cartoon storm cloud that rains only on chosen people.

Sometimes Helen walked along the sand and rooted up clumps of dry beach grass and wove stiff, useless little mats and dolls' brooms. This went on for a long time. It was more than two years after Lucy died that things began to turn.

Helen was alone in the kitchen one morning, listening to the water breathe like a baby outside, when someone knocked at the door. The loose glass pane rattled and Helen went to see who was there. It was a girl, she saw, standing and shivering in the cold. The girl had dark, eager eyes. She opened her mouth to explain herself, and a puffball of vapor came out first. The wind blew up around her and she tucked the flapping end of her mohair scarf into the top of her jacket. Helen would not let her freeze out there like the little match girl in the fairy tale. She pushed open the door and let her inside. The girl carried a huge orange valise with her, and she put it down on the hallway floor with a heavy, confident thud.

chapter seven

The woman looked older than Claire had imagined she would. Claire had knocked, and the woman had answered; it had not been difficult. She felt that the actual getting in would prove to be the hardest part, but that, too, happened with ease. The woman stood in the warmth of the house and Claire stood out in the cold. They were separated by a thin sheet of glass, and the woman obviously felt sorry for her. She pushed open the door and let Claire inside at once. Claire dropped her suitcase to the floor and stood face to face with the mother of Lucy Ascher.

She got herself in order before speaking; she brushed her hair out of her face and caught her breath. She had not been running, but she felt as though she had.

"Yes?" Helen Ascher asked. "What can I do for you?"

Claire had rehearsed what she would say, and when she

spoke, the words came out woodenly. "I wondered if you needed an au pair girl," she said. "You know, someone to clean up, and cook, and do things like that. I'm reliable."

"Well, now, I don't think so," Helen Ascher said after a moment. "The house isn't very big, and there isn't too much to clean . . . " Her voice drifted off. She seemed to be thinking about something else. It was as though Claire had interrupted her stream of thoughts, and now she was returning to it.

"Thank you," Claire mumbled, picking up her suitcase. The handle was still freezing. She was very embarrassed; the whole idea suddenly seemed idiotic. She turned to leave, but the woman's hand was on her shoulder.

"Wait," Helen Ascher said. "I didn't mean to be so hasty. Come into the kitchen where it's warmer, and we'll talk about this."

Claire followed dumbly. In high school she had had a teacher who was involved in sensitivity training and had sent his class out on what he called a "trust walk." The students were paired off—one was blindfolded, and the other one had to lead his partner around the grounds of the school. The idea was to gain trust in your peers. Claire's guide was a wise-ass kid named Rick who walked her into a tree as a joke. Now she followed once again, for the first time in years. She usually preferred to go first, to forge ahead.

The Aschers' kitchen smelled of serious cooking—none of those odors that were easy to recognize, like coffee or bacon, but more subtle smells, spices. Coriander? Claire wondered. Marjoram? Sage? They both sat down at the table, and Claire realized that Lucy must have sat there a million times in the past. Eating breakfast, doing her homework, maybe even writing poems when she got older. As Claire thought about it she began to fill with feeling, and she tried to stop these thoughts. She used to play mental games when she was all alone and had nothing to do. Don't think of the word "eggplant," she would order herself, and would try to think of other things, but naturally "eggplant" floated ridiculously in the forefront, urged on by the mere power of suggestion.

Don't think about Lucy Ascher, she told herself, but of course that was absurd. Here she was, sitting in the house in which Lucy had grown up. When she spoke to Helen Ascher, she could barely contain herself. "I must seem really weird," she said, "just showing up here like this. I mean, I guess I'm supposed to have references and things like that. I don't really know how to go about this."

Mrs. Ascher was sitting right across from her, staring at her directly, but again her thoughts seemed somewhere else. "Yes," she said in a distracted voice. "Why did you come here? This is a pretty out-of-the-way place."

Claire faltered for a second. "Just because," she answered, then quickly added, "I tried other houses in the area, I wanted a quiet place by the water. That's why I ended up here."

"I understand."

But she couldn't understand, not really. She couldn't know that Claire had left college, possibly for good, and traveled by train all day to get there. She couldn't know that Claire was in love with her daughter.

Mrs. Ascher was talking; she was saying yes, she would try

Claire out, see how things worked. She would discuss wages with her husband when he came home that day. The house could use some cleaning, after all. The garage needed to be gone through, and she was glad to have someone else to do it this year. "By the way," she said, "we don't know each other's name. Who are you?"

"Claire Danziger," she answered. She could not believe the simplicity of the situation. She was taken aback by it, startled.

"I'm Helen Ascher," the woman said, and as they shook hands Claire had difficulty keeping her expression from giving her away. Her mouth kept twitching up into a twisted version of a smile, the closest she had come to one in a long time.

That night, as she lay shaking in the guest-room bed, she tried to make sense of things. Calm down, she ordered herself, and remembered an exercise she had read about in her mother's *Redbook* magazine. It was in an article on relaxing, and one of the methods offered was to lie down on a bed and tell your body to relax, piece by piece. You were supposed to start with your head and work your way down to your feet. Neck, relax, you were supposed to say. Shoulders, relax. Ribcage, relax. By the time you reached your toes, you were supposed to be asleep. It did not work this night, but Claire was not even sure she really wanted it to. After all, here she was, lying in a bed in a house filled with history. Sleep was not necessary. In *The Bell Jar*, Plath's heroine swears to the psychiatrist that she has not slept for days, that she has spent each night watching the hands of the clock creep around the dial. After reading the book in high school for the first time, Naomi said, she went through a similar crisis. She stayed up every night, she told Claire, and spent her days walking around in a kind of manic stupor. "Manic stupor?" Claire had said. "Isn't that a paradox?"

"No," Naomi insisted. "I was all hyped up, but I didn't *do* anything at all. I was like those wind-up toys that buzz around in useless circles until they wind themselves down."

At Swarthmore, the death girls' marathon nights usually did not leave them depleted the next day. They all took naps in the afternoon and were revitalized for their next evening session. "Nobody says you have to sleep at night," Claire said once, defending herself to Julian. "What's wrong with sleeping in the daytime? In Alaska it's light all summer, and they go to sleep eventually, don't they?" Julian had said he thought they had black windowshades to keep out all the light when they wanted to go to bed.

In the guest room of the Aschers' house, the windows had white, airy curtains on them, and they hung unsashed. The room was plain and scrubbed. The walls were painted eggshell white, and the wooden floors had been polished to a high shine. The moon filled the window, and the sea rustled outside. Claire had a desire to walk along the beach in the cold, but she figured that there would be plenty of time to do things like that. Tonight, her first night, she should just lie still in bed and let everything seep slowly in. Down the hall Helen Ascher coughed. There was talking—hushed husband-and-wife talk, possibly about her.

Ray Ascher had come home from work in the late afternoon and regarded Claire with a curious expression, even after his wife had explained her presence. "I've hired Claire to do some work around the house," she told him.

"Oh," he said, "very good," but his voice was still inquisitive.

Claire felt uncomfortable. Ray Ascher was big, almost overpowering. She had not expected this. When she really thought about it, though, she could not remember what she *had* expected. She had been in a sort of daze for the past few weeks. A manic stupor, perhaps. A death-girl stupor.

Once she had made the decision to go to the house where Lucy Ascher had grown up, she packed and left Swarthmore, taking an Amtrak train from Philadelphia to New York. She tried to read during the ride—Ascher's poetry, mostly—but found that she could not concentrate. She was too nervous and kept going to the café car for food she did not want. In Penn Station she nearly changed her mind, turned around and got back on another train for Philadelphia. She could have gone directly to Julian and asked that he forgive her. He would, she knew; that was not what worried her. The problem was that she did not really want to go back to him, at least not just yet. His embrace was oddly comforting—his soft mouth, his hands. But she did not need any of that now. She required a different sort of comfort entirely.

She got out to the end of Long Island by late afternoon. The sky was overcast, and the wind was strong. Claire wandered into the local library and asked the woman behind the circulation desk for the telephone book. The place was deserted except for the librarian and an old man who was sitting at a table reading a world atlas for the longest time without turning the page. Claire wondered what part of the world could be so interesting.

The Aschers were not listed. She was stunned; she looked again, moving her index finger frantically down the page. Ascerno, Asch, Aschberger, Asche, Aschenbach, Aschner. It was missing. Blood rushed to her head, and she closed the book slowly.

"Can I help you?" the librarian asked.

Claire looked up. "I'm trying to find the Aschers' address," she said. "You know, the poet Lucy Ascher's parents. I understand they still live here. That's what I read in the introduction to Lucy Ascher's memoirs, anyway. I think they still live here. At least I hope they do. God, I came all the way out here." She was babbling now, and she stopped speaking abruptly.

The librarian smiled, showing bad teeth. "Oh yes," she said. "They still live here. It's not very far." And she gave her directions.

Claire muttered her thanks and was about to leave when the librarian added, "You may think you're the first, but you're not."

Claire turned away and hurried outside. She felt foolish; the librarian had figured out everything simply by looking at her. Am I a type? Claire wondered. In high school she had been considered a true original. There was no one else like her in the entire school, so she had naturally assumed there was no one else like her in the world. "You're a misfit!" her mother had shrieked at her once, and Claire had allowed herself to fall further into the role, beginning to see its advantages. People left you alone if you were a misfit, and you were able to do and say as you pleased. Claire would sit at the back of the classroom, leaning her chair against the wall, never listening to the lesson, openly reading Lucy Ascher's poetry or else writing some of her own. The teachers noticed but never said anything, because Claire performed stellarly on tests and papers. One day she was called into the school psychologist's office. Apparently one of Claire's teachers had requested the evaluation; she never found out which one it was, although she suspected her young male math teacher, who occasionally had a copy of *Psychology Today* on his desk to read during lunch hour. The meeting was short. Mrs. Melcher, a heavy, kindly woman, seemed delighted with Claire and ended up telling her she should not think of herself as "different"—she should think of herself as "special." Somehow this advice did not carry her through life. She was still restless, still looking.

Claire found the Aschers' house easily. It was large and plain, and an old paneled station wagon was parked out front. She was very cold, and she wished she had remembered to bring a pair of gloves with her. Someone was moving around inside the house, she could see through the window. A couple of times she wanted to turn around, but the wind pushed her forward. Okay, she thought, this is really it. There was no doorbell, so she knocked. The glass pane shook at her touch, and she was afraid she had knocked too hard, that the glass would fall to the ground and splinter. But nothing happened and no one came to the door. She wondered then if perhaps she had not knocked hard enough.

The wind blew up a small leaf-and-sand storm in her face,

and as she put up her hand to protect her eyes, she could hear someone coming. She tucked in her scarf, and the wind immediately loosened it once again. The mother of Lucy Ascher was looking straight at her through the glass and then, after what seemed like a full minute of deliberation, she pushed open the door and let Claire inside where it was warm.

Her chores were minimal from the very start. "Oh," Helen Ascher said, waving her hand vaguely, "just dust this area because Ray is pretty allergic."

Claire was given a cardboard box filled with cleaning supplies: a feather duster, a couple of aerosol cans, some old rags which had once been undershirts, and a few special attachments for the vacuum cleaner. She was looking forward to the idea of physical labor; it was something that she had not really done before. At home her responsibilities had been few. Her mother had always yelled at her to pitch in, to get moving, but then when Claire actually did help out, her mother shooed her away. She could not stand it when the house was not in perfect shape, and she did not trust anyone else to do the job. "I have to take care of everything around here," she would say.

"Is there anything I can do?" Claire would ask, but she already knew the answer.

"Oh, you," her mother would say, "you'd just create a bigger mess. You and your father are exactly alike. Go into the other room and make yourself scarce for a while."

Claire tried to think—had things always been that way? She could not remember. She certainly had had some fun when she was a child. There were photographs that served as fair proof: Claire and Seth at the Catskills Game Farm, petting a fat lamb with yellowed fleece, smiles on their faces, circa 1966. Claire and Seth and Dad huddling over a hibachi, their faces wavy in the heat at a backyard barbecue, circa 1968. Their mother had taken the picture; her thumb blotted out one third of it. When the roll of film came back from Kodak, they probably kidded her about being a "lousy shutterbug." There must have been some close times; every family has them.

She tried to get a sense of the Aschers' family life, but it was very difficult to do. Both Helen and Ray were reserved people. Sometimes Ray offered comments about his classes during dinner, but even then his voice was low and inexpressive. In the second chapter of *Sleepwalking*, Lucy wrote that Ray was "a large, brooding father. There always seemed to be too much of him. His shoes were so huge that when I was a kid I used to hide all eight of my hamsters in a single Oxford, then lace it up, put my hand over it and listen to the muted squeals and thrashing inside."

To Claire, Ray Ascher appeared to be a hulking man who filled rooms with his oppressive sadness, like a buffalo knowing dimly that it is of a dying breed and nothing can be done to save it. But that part of him was probably something that surfaced only after his daughter's death. Lucy could not have known what would happen after she died, although Claire thought she must have tried to imagine. Wasn't that a universal fantasy—trying to guess what would happen after you died, how your loved ones would react? In a moment of thrilling self-pity, doesn't everyone try to imagine solemn friends and family at graveside?

When Claire took Driver's Education in high school, her instructor handed everyone a pamphlet entitled *Hey, I'm Too Young to Die!* It was written in the first person. "What are you doing?" it began. "C'mon, you guys, let me out of here. It's cold in this coffin." It was supposed to be told from the point of view of a careless teenage driver who had been killed in a collision. "Hey, Mom," it read, "and Dad, and Sis, and Peewee, don't look so sad, huh? Grandma, I can't stand to see you cry. Please, just get it over with already. Reverend, finish up the prayers. I can't take much more of this!"

Claire thought that if a person were able to look into the future and take a quick peek at a videotape of his own funeral, he would enjoy the remainder of his life more fully. He would hear the extent of the moaning and the keening and would, perhaps for the first time ever, feel well and truly loved. Claire sometimes wondered if her parents really loved her. She supposed that they must, in that perfunctory, parental way that is taken for granted by children, but real love, in Claire's mind, required something additional.

Julian tried his hardest to love her. He was tender, certainly, and he was filled with passion. She thought of him, and as she did she realized that she did miss him. She felt oddly safe when they were together. Now she was out on the end of Long Island in this strange, rickety house, and she no longer felt safe. Claire believed in extremes, believed in carrying things as far as they would go, but now she wondered if she had overdone it. She suddenly wanted the easy peace of her own bedroom at Swarthmore, with Julian's slim, warm body lying against hers. On the first night at the Aschers', after the exercises did not work, she lay awake and rigid for a long time.

In the very middle of the night, when the moon hesitated in the sky, Claire felt an odd sensation. It was as though someone were giving her the chills up and down her back. At summer camp she and her bunkmates used to give each other the chills all day long. There was even a chant you were supposed to repeat as you languidly grazed your fingers in various formations along a friend's back. "X marks the spot," the chant began, "with a dash and a dot, and a pinch and a squeeze, and a cool ocean breeze." At the last words you were supposed to blow lightly on the other person's neck, to heighten and finalize the "chill."

Claire felt it as she lay there—the brushing of fingers, all along her back and across her shoulders. She shivered and sat up in bed. There seemed to be a definite presence in the room, a form of some kind. Surprisingly, it was not an unpleasant feeling. Claire did not turn on the light or move. She looked around her, barely turning her head; the door was still shut all the way, as she had left it, and so was the window. The closet had not been opened, and nothing stirred under the bed. Helen and Ray Ascher had stopped talking hours earlier, and there was no noise anywhere in the house. Claire was not dreaming, and she knew her feeling was real: It occurred to her, after several minutes of pure stillness, what it must be. The presence in the room, voiceless and shapeless, was obviously the ghost of Lucy Ascher.

"Hello?" Claire said into the darkness. The sound of her

own voice usually embarrassed her when she was alone. She hated talking into those telephone-answering machines. On this night, though, her voice pleased her. She spoke into the darkness once again. "Lucy?" she said, and she did not feel at all self-conscious. Maybe, she thought, that was because she did not feel alone. She felt as if Lucy Ascher were sitting across the room in the wicker rocker, keeping vigil like a night nurse. Just sitting by herself, asking for nothing, like a solid friend. "I know you're there," Claire said. The chill draped over her grandly now. She felt herself becoming drowsy underneath it, as if it were an anesthetic. The last thing she remembered seeing that night was the outline of the rocking chair. She was not positive, but before she fell asleep she thought she saw it rock lightly forward and then back again, all by itself.

Because Helen Ascher had no real idea of what had to be done in the house, Claire wandered around on her own the next day, looking for things that needed cleaning or fixing. She walked through the rooms like a visitor in a museum, touching furniture as though it were illegal to do so. When she was younger she liked to run her hand surreptitiously along the edges of certain paintings in the Metropolitan so she could have the satisfaction of thinking, I touched where Picasso touched. Years later she thought this childhood desire had larger implications: maybe she had really been trying to make some contact, to feel a kinship with a person who moved her. In the museum her father would stand, flicking out his wrist to stare at his watch and tapping his foot against the smooth floor of the gallery. Claire would take in as many colors as she could before her parents whisked her away.

The Aschers' house looked as if people had enjoyed living there once, a long time ago. Claire sensed that many parties had been held—marine biology department parties, perhaps. There was a neat oval wine stain on one corner of the beige living-room rug, but it was very faded. Claire played paleon-tologist; she estimated that the stain was at least ten years old. She could feel the thrust of that ancient party, could see a professor let his glass slip from his hand in the midst of an overly spirited conversation. Everyone must automatically have hunched over to look, murmuring things, offering different wine-stain remedies—a dab of glycerine, a teaspoon of white wine to counteract the red. The professor's wife probably hur-ried into the kitchen to gather a ball of paper towels. The husband and wife most likely left the party early that night.

There was a cigarette burn on the surface of the rock-maple coffee table—a perfect circle, like a bullet hole. The guests at the Aschers' parties must have been very wrapped up in their talk. There had been an energy in the house years ago, of that Claire was sure. Ray and Helen had sat downstairs with their friends at a lively, noisy party while upstairs in their daughter's room something brewed, and they knew nothing about it.

Claire's parents never entertained anymore. There had often been parties when Claire and Seth were small children. Claire had loved the hum and festivity in the house. Her mother would give each of them a plateful of pigs-in-blankets to take back upstairs. The television set would be left on for them to watch as late as they liked, but there was never anything good

on Saturday nights, and she and Seth spent the evening running back and forth between their rooms and the party. One
of her father's friends, a man she had never liked, would invari-
ably catch her up in his arms as she ran past. "Aha, gotcha!"
he would say, as if he had made a conquest. One time he and
his wife had just returned from a tour of Europe, and he told
Claire to ask him anything about Europe she wished. Claire
had learned about foreign countries in school that year, but
her family had not yet been any farther away than Williams-
burg, Virginia.

"Come on," the man prodded in front of everyone. "Ask
me something, or I won't let you go."

He smelled of hair tonic, a sweetness made foul by the
excess of it, and Claire wanted to get away. "Okay," she finally
said. "Do animals in Europe make the same sounds as the ones
here?" It was a question she had seriously wondered about.

Her parents' friends broke up over this. "Where did you *get*
her?" the man asked, placing his large hand flat on the top of
Claire's head. She ducked and squirmed away from him.

Years later the parties came to an eternal halt when her
parents found out Seth had leukemia. Or maybe it was even
earlier than that, when Seth was tired all the time, and they
sensed instinctively that something was wrong. Everyone else
in the family became tired, too. When Seth said good night
at nine, said that he was beat, it was not long before her mother
began to yawn and stretch, and then her father did the same.
"Might as well all turn in early," her father would say, as if in
explanation. Claire would stay up for a few minutes longer,
sitting by herself in the dim kitchen.

From the time Seth got sick until a week before he died, there was a feeling of solemn quiet in the Danzigers' house. It was a terrible hush that to an outsider might have appeared tranquil. An artist would have been very happy working and living in the house; it was quiet and painstakingly clean and the back windows offered northern exposure.

But there was no real peace to be had. Inside her parents, little storms waited to rage, in each heart a thunderclap. When the family left for Italy, Claire could feel it all beginning to surface on the airplane. Her father refused to let her rent a set of earphones so she could listen to the movie; he said it was a waste of money. She sat in her usual spot by the window. The plane was lifting up over the airport and Queens, and Claire felt the widening space between herself and the roofs below.

Her father ordered some Scotch, and when the stewardess did not bring it for several minutes, he became impatient, then nasty. "Jesus," he said aloud, "this is pretty crappy service around here, even if it is only tourist class." Claire pressed her face closer to the window, her mouth open on the glass, as if for air.

During the flight her mother switched seats a lot, looking for better leg room, and her father took occasional swigs from a bottle of Maalox he had brought with him in his flight bag. His lips were rimmed in white. The family ate dinner in complete silence, and after the meal was over, her father switched off all three of the overhead reading lights.

On the screen, the movie had just begun. Passengers watched and listened with their earphones looped docilely under their chins. Claire looked at the screen for a while, trying to read lips, but she soon grew bored with this. She was going out of the country for the very first time; the airplane was at that moment rushing over the Atlantic Ocean. She felt as though it did not matter where she was headed. It was understood that her family was traveling to Europe not for the purpose of seeing anything new, but rather to get away from the old. Claire decided she would make her body go limp and let herself be freely transported anywhere—to Europe, to a distant planet, or right back to her living room to stare at the little dents that had been left in the carpet after the furniture had been moved during the shiva period. She wasn't positive, but she didn't think anyone had remembered to move it back. Claire would let herself be taken along without asking questions. She had absolutely no preference of place. When it came time to choose a college, it did not really matter to her where she went. She had been offered financial aid by Swarthmore, Duke, Cornell and Stanford. It was her mother who had looked through all of the catalogues and decided for her. "You want a small school," she said, "where you're not just a number in a computer."

That was why it was odd for Claire to find herself, two years later, in the house of Helen and Ray Ascher. It was *she* who had decided to go there, *she* who had realized it was the place she needed to be. Claire stood alone in the center of the Aschers' sloping den with a feather duster in her hand, its plumage sprouting upward like a thriving plant.

chapter eight

True or false: A mollusk is an invertebrate animal with a soft, unsegmented body that is usually contained in a calcareous shell.

Oh, true.

He had come home from giving a quiz to a large, vacant-looking group of freshmen that afternoon, and she had been there, sitting at the kitchen table. Helen looked up at him pointedly, as though to transmit the message: *I'll explain later*. Ray sat down in the chair across from Claire and studied her. She blinked a few times and tapped her fingers in a rhythmless pattern on the tabletop. He wondered if it was remotely possible that he made her nervous. Ray was fairly sure that he had never made anyone nervous before in his life.

He listened patiently as Helen explained that they would be trying out Claire as a live-in maid for a while. Things needed to be done around the house, she said, and she herself did not have the energy to do them. It would be nice to have a little spring cleaning done, to have the place in order once again, didn't he think? Ray nodded in agreement, and thought that the three of them certainly made a motley crew. They looked like people sitting in the waiting room of a pain clinic, each person's pain manifesting itself in a different way, but the message being driven home all the same.

Helen showed it in her constant distractedness. You could sustain a conversation with her for only a limited time. Despair had enclosed her completely over the past few years. She was distracted in everything she did. Sometimes she forgot to shut off the flame under boiling soups, under macaroni, filling the kitchen with rich, rolling smoke and blackening the bottoms of pots. He wondered what had held them together since Lucy's death. Maybe it would have been easier if they had separated and lived alone, or if each had lived with someone new, someone hopeful and life-giving.

Ray often wondered what kept people together as couples, as lovers. Was it the sharing of so many burdens—growing old, unpaid mortgages, concern over a child's fever? Or was it simply the endless slapping together of bellies in the night, the routine of practiced lovemaking? He knew he was not the best of lovers. "There is too much of you," Helen had said to him once. "I can't even put my arms all the way around you." She had laughed while saying it, but occasionally he wondered if she saw him as only a floating hunk of driftwood that took up three quarters of their king-sized bed. Such a big, strong brute, and he couldn't manage to set things right again. He tried over and over to console her, but the attempts were always awkward and forced and useless. Even a Saint Bernard, as dumb and as big, a flask of brandy strapped to its neck, had better instincts.

There was something to be said for self-preservation, though. Ray had to keep himself from real depression however best he could. He stayed long hours at the lab, even longer than Stan Bergman, the most dedicated and neurotic person in the entire department. Sometimes in the late evening the two men would be the only ones left working in the building. Even the janitor would have gone home for the night, whistling as he wheeled his rumbling trash barrel down the hallway. Once in a while Stan would suggest that he and Ray go out for a drink after they were each through with their work, but Ray always put it off and they never got around to it.

He had long ago forgotten the dynamics of one-to-one conversation. With Helen, he did most of the talking, as well as most of the listening, too, he believed. He declined to teach a small senior seminar on early forms of aquatic life because he knew that such a course would require hours of private conferences with students, and he did not think he could handle that. He had no idea of what to say to them when they came to him with particular problems. He stuck with teaching huge lecture classes with spot quizzes and little interaction with students. He kept infrequent office hours and sometimes didn't even answer the door when someone knocked. He would sit completely still, pretending he was not there, and soon a note would be nudged under the door and the person would go away.

Ray's pain showed itself in his immutable stiffness, and also lately in his bulk. He ate a lot more, choosing foods he did not even especially like. In the faculty cafeteria he ordered plates of baked ziti and squash, and yellow and green Jello-O jewels for dessert. He drank several cups of coffee with each meal, thinking it would step things up inside him, but all it did was make him climb the stairs to the third-floor men's toilet more often than usual.

His colleagues left him alone. They knew, and they did not want to delve, sensing it would be an intrusion. They smiled at him and slapped him lightly on the back when they passed him in the hall. He was invited to all of the faculty sherry hours, but he never went. He preferred to stay in the laboratory, where things were bright and noiseless and smelled of the chemicals he had been inhaling in that very room for years.

Unlike Helen, he was not in the least distracted; he could easily spend hours with his head dipped over the microscope, observing a specimen he especially liked. He was fascinated by detail—he increased the magnification of the lens and closely studied the little rows of ridges on a starfish's arm. He enjoyed toying with the focus so that what he saw became clear and then clouded, then clear once again. It reminded him of the tiny, dark room at the Museum of Modern Art where you could sit all day and watch a screen on which colors blend and then are clarified.

One of the things Ray had liked best about his marriage was the fact that he and Helen were involved in the same field. They would lie in bed at night, turning the pages of an over-sized glossy book on the ocean. That was all over now; Helen's interest in marine biology had, he thought wryly, ebbed. It was funny how many of the phrases that came to mind when thinking of his own life were somehow sea-related. *Her interest had ebbed. They were both drowning in their sorrow. He had sunk lower than ever before.* The vocabulary of the ocean seemed tailored to loss.

It was no longer their work that bound them, but still, he and Helen were somehow oddly joined. They were drawn together by a shared sadness, and that was as good a reason to stay together as any Ray could think of. They did small things for each other. Late at night they would take turns giving back rubs. Helen was good at this—she would press her fingers and knuckles deep into the areas of tension she had isolated in his neck and shoulders. He sometimes wondered if there was a certain amount of anger behind such a stern, almost vicious rubdown, but he never questioned it, because it felt nice. When it was his turn to massage Helen, he would open his large hands flat and move them slowly up and down her back, applying just a little pressure and some sweet-smelling body pomade. He could not bear the thought of causing her any pain.

On Saturdays they worked around the house, doing odd jobs. They cleaned out the small guest bathroom together, barely both fitting into such a small space. Helen would bend down over the tub while Ray wiped the countertops. They were constantly bumping into each other by accident—elbows, thighs, even heads. Once when this happened he thought sadly that it was one of the only times they had touched each other spontaneously for a long time. They still made love—not very often, but occasionally, when the dinner was fine, and the night was cold, and they had not taken any interesting books out of the library that week. "Do you want to?" he would ask, and she would respond simply by beginning to unbutton her blouse and turning back the covers on the bed. He wanted to stop her, to tell her she should not sleep with him for his benefit, but he could not bring himself to. He was not really sure how she felt about it.

Helen was quite beautiful at fifty-five, and he thought she would probably remain that way for several more years. She was thin and held herself well, as she always had. She wore casual clothing every day—soft flannel shirts and slacks. Over the years she had let her hair grow very long, but she always kept it tied up in a loose knot at the back of her head. There was a good deal of gray laced in with the blond now. When Lucy was very little and had been especially trying, Helen would roll her eyes and say to Ray, "This is why parents get gray." He would laugh, but now he realized that there had been some truth to this explanation.

It *was* children who did it, who drained the life from you, who made you run around the room playing piggyback until you were out of breath. It was children who scared you as no other people could. The first time Lucy had tried to kill herself and Ray had been called ashore by the local Coast Guard, he had seen Helen standing all alone on the dock, clutching herself tightly, and he had known without any doubt that it was about Lucy. He had been able to tell from the urgency of the way Helen stood, and when he got off the boat he had slipped into her arms and wanted to stay there forever.

They were a pair now, when once they had been part of a trio, if you could really have called it that. People came to visit them, but it was clear that no one else fit into the setting. The Wassermans, a cheerful young couple from down the road, sometimes came over with a huge pot of bouillabaisse and sat mooning at each other all evening. They had been married for just under a year, and they were very much in love. As they sat in the Aschers' living room, smiling and looking incongruously radiant in the midst of the gloom, Ray thought that the scene should have been captioned: *What is wrong with this picture?*

The day he came home from the laboratory and saw the girl sitting on one of the kitchen chairs, dressed in a black turtle-neck, her face pale, looking as though she were about to blow apart, the first thing that occurred to him was how well she *fit*. It was as though she really belonged there. He did not know who she was, but it was clear that she was in very great pain. He put down his briefcase and took off his mittens with his teeth, the way he had done since he was a child. A last remnant of the cold took hold of him, and he said a perfunctory "Brrr" and rubbed his palms together.

Helen explained the girl's presence, and he quickly agreed that she should stay. He stared at Claire, watched as her dark eyes blinked and she sat upright and tense in her chair. He wondered, then, if she was possibly one of the lonelies, the crazies. One of the groupies.

That night in bed, he confronted Helen. She was lying on her back in a thin pink nightgown—a little out of season, he thought. He could see her breasts through the fabric. "Helen," he said to her, "why is she really here, do you think?"

She turned to him. "I'm not sure what you mean by that," she said.

"You know," he said. "Do you think she knows about things?"

Helen sighed. "I guess," she said. "It doesn't matter too much, does it? She seems responsible."

Ray paused, then he asked, "Does the house really need extra cleaning?"

"I wouldn't hire her if it didn't," Helen said. "What are you getting at?"

"She seems troubled, and sad, in a way. I just thought you might have felt sorry for her or something . . . I don't know what I mean. Forget it; it's very late."

She did not say anything in response. She had probably begun to think of other things already. They kissed, and her lips were dry and warm. Afterward she turned away from him, positioned for sleep. Ray thought about the girl Claire as he lay next to his wife. He kept envisioning her large, frightened eyes, her death mask of a face. There was something compelling about her. It all seemed logical to him when he thought about it. She had come to the door, and Helen had let her in. She probably was one of the lonelies, one of those who telephoned late and sobbed into the receiver, but if so, she was of a different sort than any he had seen or spoken to before. She had come to the house not to gawk, not to interview anyone, but because, he supposed, she had recognized it as a kind of sanctuary. Actually, the house *was* a sanctuary, even to him. He felt comfortable nowhere else.

The winter before, he and Helen had decided to go away for a weekend. They made reservations at an inn in New Hampshire that dated back to 1770. The room they were given was spacious and quiet, with a working fireplace and a very high antique canopy bed. The wallpaper was peppered all over with tiny blue cornflowers. Everything was beautiful and peaceful, but an hour after they arrived, Ray began to feel anxious. Where was the sea? There was no water anywhere for miles and miles. He began to panic. He opened the window shades in the room and saw that the views from all three oversized windows were dominated by mountains—solid, oppressive snowcaps. He sat down on the bed, under the shade of its canopy. Helen was unpacking toiletries in the bathroom. He heard her slide the medicine chest open and then try the hot and cold faucets to make sure they didn't run rust.

"Come see the bathtub," she called. "It has those wonderful curlicue feet on it." When he did not respond, she poked her head out of the doorway. She saw him sitting on the bed, sweating. He put his hand up to his head. "Are you sick, sweetie?" Helen asked, and he realized that those were the very words she had said the day Lucy stopped talking, more than ten years earlier. Or at least it was the way Lucy had remembered and recounted them in her journal.

"I feel really dizzy," he said. He knew it was pure anxiety; he had experienced the same sort of feeling two other times in his life. The first time was when he was locked for too long a time in a tight hold during wrestling practice in college and thought he was about to suffocate. The second time was right after he saw the Holocaust documentary film *Night and Fog.*

This was the worst, though. The other two times he had actually derived a little thrill from hearing people say, "Give him air," as they pressed his head down into the space between

his knees. There was something different about a fat man faint-
ing. It was the unexpected—obese people were like those
delicately weighted little toys that are designed never to topple.
When the elephant in the circus gets to its great wrinkled
knees, everyone cranes to look.

They left the inn that very evening; he said he could not
bear to stay any longer. Helen drove them home, and he apologized profusely throughout the ride. They got back to Southampton seven hours later, in the middle of the night. He
simply could not leave his natural habitat. He felt like those
children who are born without resistance to germs and have
to spend their whole lives in the controlled environment of a
plastic tent, and whose visitors have to wear beekeeper outfits.

The idea of captivity was not a new one to Ray. He had
read so many animal books when he was a kid in Brooklyn,
and the plot was always roughly the same: boy finds wounded
wild animal, nurses it back to health and keeps it as a household pet; soon the animal becomes unhappy and listless, and
the boy's father tells him, in a really intense father-son dis-
course, that the animal needs to go back to its natural habitat.
So the boy tearfully sets "Bandit" free, and the book draws to
a close.

There was supposed to be nothing as good as freedom. But
what if your natural environment was captivity to begin with?
Where did that leave you? Certainly the small house on Cobb's
Lane was oppressive, with its peeling paint and leftover air of
mourning. But even so, it served as a sanctuary. Ray could sit
in the den with a glass of vodka and a plate of hot food, listening to the sounds of the ocean and not having to talk to anyone.

Helen must feel that way about the house too, he thought, or else she wouldn't spend all her time there. She went into town as infrequently as she could. Being recognized as the mother of Lucy Ascher was only a problem during the summer, when the season was in full swing. Then people often turned and looked at her when she went shopping in the local supermarket. They had seen the photographs in the middle of *Lucy Ascher: Portrait of a Dreamer*, the critical biography that had come out a few months before, and knew that the Aschers still lived in Southampton. There was a full-page picture in the book of Helen and Ray with Lucy sitting between them. It was taken the afternoon she had received a special award from the American Academy of Arts and Letters, the spring before her death. Helen and Ray were wearing light-colored clothing, and Lucy was wearing a heavy, dark dress. They made a striking group.

Nobody ever actually bothered Helen or Ray when they went into town; they just looked, and nudged each other and whispered. After a while you got used to it. Even so, it was good to have a place of refuge, and the house provided that. Helen carried this to an extreme; she stayed indoors and did nothing all day. She had become useless. Lately she had taken to collecting supermarket coupons and to stringing leaves of dried beach grass into little ornaments that littered the mantelpiece. "Why don't you get out more?" Ray suggested once. "Physical exercise feels good. I read somewhere that it can help make you less depressed."

They decided they would start jogging the very next morning. They woke at sunrise and dressed together in the dark room. "This had better be worth it," she said in a groggy voice as she bent to tie the shoelace of her Nikes.

They ran side by side along the beach, kicking up sand behind them. At first it was easy; the morning air was wet and cold, and Ray inhaled deeply, feeling as though he were slowly being purified. The house was set on a long strip of sand, and they decided they would jog until the beach ended. "How are you doing?" he called to her periodically over the screech of gulls.

"Just fine," she answered, looking straight ahead. She ran stiffly, barely moving her arms. Her breathing started to come with effort soon, although she seemed to be trying not to let it show. She breathed through her nose only, the proper way, but her nostrils flared with each new, labored intake of air. "Do you want to stop and rest awhile?" he asked her once when they were approaching a large piece of driftwood that would have served as a nice bench.

She shook her head resolutely and did not say anything. Ray was barely winded at all. He was in fairly good shape for a man as heavy as he. It had something to do with his wrestling coach back at City College, who always insisted that team members get some sort of extra physical activity each day. It took Ray some time to decide what it was he should do. He immediately ruled out swimming because he was embarrassed by his paleness, and the harsh white lights over the pool made him feel all the more exposed. He ended up lifting weights, coming to the gym each day an hour before his first class, in order to work out. His arms became corded, and his chest began to feel more dense. After college he continued to lift heavy things, liking the way the veins in his arms became prominent when he strained to pick up a color TV, or a carton of textbooks for his class.

As he ran with Helen he felt he could continue at the same pace for several miles. He almost wished the beach didn't end after the yellow house. A feeling of confidence rushed through him, and he began to run faster. "Is this too much for you?" he yelled to Helen, and she shook her head, even though it was clear that she was having a hard time of it. As long as she didn't complain, he would not stop. His legs moved with precision, like well-oiled machine parts. He could almost hear them make a whirring sound.

It could not last. They were still going along well, at an even, quick trot, when Ray began to feel out of breath. He tried to ignore the feeling, but he couldn't. Sometimes in the early morning he would wake with a full bladder but be too tired to get out of bed. He would fall back into sleep and dream that he had gotten up and urinated in a great arc. He would wake again seconds later and realize that his bladder was still full. You could not fool the body.

He glanced at Helen and saw that she had begun to breathe through her mouth. It was wide open and she was gasping like a caught fish. They both slowed down at the same time, and their steps, without the aid of speed, turned clumsy. They began to kick up sand in huge, careless sprays. Ray knew he would have to stop, and just as he realized this, he caught sight of the young couple from down the road. The Wassermans were jogging gracefully toward Ray and Helen, wearing identical sweat suits, royal blue with gold racing stripes lining the sides. Their faces were vibrant and flushed, and they were rib-bing each other playfully as they ran.

"Ha!" she called to him. "You can't do much more, Mike!"

"Oh, yeah?" he called back. "Let's see who sticks it out longer!"

Then they laughed and hugged each other for a moment, still moving. They soon passed Ray and Helen and smiled and waved and called out "Good morning!" The Wassermans were thin and blond and graceful. Ray thought they looked like Hitler's ideal of Aryan youth. As he watched the couple go by, he suddenly felt hopeless about his own life. He looked over at Helen and saw that she was openly wheezing. They were both moving at an embarrassingly slow pace now. "Oh," he said at last, reaching for her arm, "let's stop."

They collapsed on the beach, a few inches from the water. The Wassermans were almost completely out of sight now. The foot-prints they had left behind in the damp sand were delicate and unassuming, like the tracks birds leave. Ray felt heavy and awful and, most of all, old. When you reached your fifties, things moved faster but took a lot more effort. If your body didn't slow you down, your thoughts did. Just the other night he had been brushing his teeth over the sink, and in the middle he had started to think about Lucy and the time when there were three Aschers and he and Helen had loved each other fiercely. He didn't realize it, but he stopped brushing his teeth and began to daydream about the early years of his marriage. He was standing there motionless for several minutes, holding his dripping brush poised over the basin, his mouth still slathered with toothpaste, when Helen passed by the bathroom and saw him.

"Ray," she said. "What are you doing?" He had come instantly to life again when she spoke, back to the sorry life that was his own. He rinsed out his mouth and went to bed.

He came to expect that as he got older there would be many more moments of this kind of stoppage. He experienced one of them as he lay sprawled out on the beach with Helen, trying to breathe. It was a long while until they were both recovered enough to get up and start back toward home. They walked slowly. Ray still faltered and wheezed, and Helen had a stitch in her side. They supported each other as they made their way to the house.

People were always extolling the virtues of growing old alongside someone you love. If this was what it entailed, Ray wanted no part of it. He had too much pride to display his inertia to another person, even to Helen. He would rather grow old alone, in some seedy hotel. This was only another one of his many dismal fantasies; he knew that in reality he would never leave her. He loved Helen, and besides, he figured that an inert personality such as his could not make major changes. There would be no flux in Ray's life other than the inevitable slow process of aging. He would stay where he was, alone with his wife, with the sea thundering outside.

Claire fit into this life of stagnation with ease. If she had been an average girl—a sweet, well-adjusted college kid looking to make a few dollars so she and a friend could go hear some rock concert—he would have pulled her aside and said, "Look, you don't want to work for us. We're not happy people."

But he understood at once that she wasn't a happy person either, so he said nothing.

As the days passed, Ray realized that he liked having Claire around. He would forget that she was there, and then, as he went into the kitchen to have his breakfast, he would see her at the sink, unloading the dishwasher from last night's dinner. "Hello," she would say to him, never "Good morning." He sensed that she was one of those people who, when someone said "Good morning" to her, would reply, "What's so good about it?" And she would mean it. At nineteen, Claire Danziger looked as though her life were over.

Lucy had looked that way most of the time. Even in sleep her face had been tragic. He had come into Lucy's room late one night because he thought he had left his reading glasses there, and he had seen her and known then that she never relaxed. Her mouth and eyes were screwed tight, dampness matted tendrils of hair to her neck. Ray had felt a kind of paternal ache, but he could not express it. Lucy would not allow it; she always kept herself at a safe distance from both her parents. She had learned early to be independent. Once when she was a very little girl, Ray had watched as she tried to teach herself to tie her shoes. Her small hands fumbled with the thick red laces, and finally she created some semblance of a bow. At the age of four she had showed a real desire to read. She would take down one of Ray and Helen's books from the shelf in the den and pretend to read, whispering made-up words as she ran her finger along the page and squinted her eyes in a good imitation of concentration.

So they pushed her ahead, indulging her with the

independence she wanted. On her door was a glow-in-the-dark sign that read: "Keep Out! This Means You!" They smiled when they saw it and allowed her many hours of solitude. She had no social graces at all. She did not know how to talk with anyone, how to share things. "Leave me alone," she would say whenever her parents touched her.

Her aloofness was a constant state, but sometimes when her guard was down she let her parents see that she was in pain. She would sit and tremble and refuse to talk about what was troubling her. "What can the matter be?" Ray and Helen would ask each other. They telephoned Lucy's fourth-grade teacher every few weeks to find out if perhaps something upsetting had happened in school to make Lucy miserable. No, the teacher always patiently reported, everything went smoothly that day. The children had learned how plants get the water they need in order to grow. They had dipped stalks of celery into shallow dishes of red ink and had observed later in the morning how the ink had begun to climb up the pale veins in the stalk. Lucy had taken part in the experiment like all of the other children. She had not seemed troubled. The teacher told Ray and Helen not to worry, that Lucy was merely shy, that she would soon emerge from her shell.

But the shell was hard—calcareous, Ray thought, like a mollusk's. Such a tough, thick shell to protect such a soft, slight interior. You could dissect a mollusk; you could splay it open on a slide and look at it for hours. You could delve into the very heart of its softness and see what was there. It would make life easier if people were like that, if you could try to figure them out while they were in an open, yielding state. Most people were born with self-protection devices that didn't allow you to go near, to explore. It had been that way with Lucy. It seemed to be that way with the girl Claire. She was completely closed off, snug inside her shell. She stood in the kitchen early each morning, putting away plates and glasses and silver, wordless except for a brief greeting. She would speak, he guessed, when she had something to say.

But he did not want to wait. He was suddenly curious about her, without understanding why. Maybe it was the father in him—he had always been curious when Lucy brought a friend to the house, which was not very often. "So," he would say, "you're in Lucy's class. Do you enjoy school? What's your favorite subject?" The child would stare back blankly.

Maybe it was the father in him, and maybe it was the scientist. As far as he was concerned, everything unfolded back to that little mollusk. What a wonderful cracking sound when your thumbs dug in to pull back the flaps of the opaque shell like a tiny curtain—the sound of discovery.

chapter nine

Dear Claire,

Where are you when we need you? It's getting to be that time of year again—the heart of winter, when, as you once said, "the lemming inside me" takes over. I really do feel depressed these days. Life at Swarthmore is as grim as ever. None of my classes are worth my time, with the possible exception of modern dance, which I'm not even getting credit for. For some reason, I actually like being around those snot-nosed danseuses, the ones with the really long braids and sucked-in cheeks and rosin all over their hands from hours spent gripping the barre. Do you remember that girl Francesca who lived on my floor last year, the one who drank liquid protein all the time and went around freshman week telling everyone how she'd gotten accepted to the Joffrey but had decided to go to Swarthmore instead, so she could be a more "whole person"?

She's in this class, and she's been whispering to everyone how weird I am, and how weird you and Laura are, too. It seems that everyone knows you've left school. It's the great mystery on campus, what happened to you. Everyone expects us to be in threes all the time.

I mean it when I say we need you. I need you, at any rate. I'm getting a little worried about Laura. She's as depressed as always, but something's different. On Friday I found her sitting out in the snow very late at night. We were supposed to meet to see Psycho, *and she never showed up. I looked around for a long time, but I couldn't find her. Later that night I went out to get a Tab, and she was just sitting there, in a small bank of snow in front of my dorm, waiting for me. She swore that she'd been sitting there for over an hour, but I'm pretty sure she was exaggerating. Wouldn't she have turned blue and started to get frostbite if she'd been there that long? I think she just wanted attention, which I immediately gave her. She came inside and we talked for a few hours. She seemed really spaced-out, and I'm not sure what's going on. I wish you had been here; you would have known what to do.*

I saw Julian Gould the other day. I was on my way to the library and was carrying a huge stack of books on the Enlightenment, and he came sprinting up to me from all the way across the campus. I think he must wear a Geiger counter around his neck; he always seems to conveniently show up whenever I come outside. He was Mr. Congeniality, and he practically grabbed the books from my hands. He asked the same questions about you all over again, like when were you planning on coming back to school, and did you mention him at all in your letter to me and Laura. When I refused to tell him anything, he asked if we could play Twenty Questions about you, and then he would leave me alone. It was odd— I felt sorry for him. He seems very lonely. As I stood there refusing to give away any information, I suddenly lost sight of what this is all about anyway. It seemed so bizarre that I have to cover for you. I mean, I'm glad that you took this step—I don't think I would have the courage to do the same thing—but I wish you would finish up soon.

I wanted to know a couple of things that you neglected to mention in your letter. The obvious one is this: Do the Aschers know why you're there yet, and if so, how do they feel about it? I saw a photograph of them in that fat biography of Lucy that's in the bookstore, and I thought they looked really formidable. Are they? Your letter was full of gaps.

I'm awed that all of this has happened so easily. I was positive you would be back at school a day or so after you left. I know that Laura and I encouraged you to do this, but frankly, I had no idea that it would turn out to be an extended thing. I'm sure that if I had approached Aurelia Plath the day I sat and watched her from across the street, she would have been able to tell right away what I was doing there, and she would have turned and walked away from me. My face always gives me away. Yours does too, you know. Are you absolutely sure the Aschers don't know what you're doing there? Maybe they really do, but are just being silent about it. Even so, I can't imagine why they would just let you stay *like that, with no references, no experience, no anything, except charm. You never cease to amaze me, Claire.*

I have to end this letter soon, Laura's about to come over for a meeting. There's something lifeless about the sessions when you're not at them. That time before Christmas, when you were with Julian all the time, our sessions just dragged without you. Laura resented the fact that you didn't think it was important to show up, but I felt more sad than angry. However different Laura and I feel, I think we both agree that something basic is missing when you're not here. At our meeting last night, neither one of us wanted to start things off. It was like the beginning of Marty: "What do you want to do?" . . . "I don't know, what do you want to do?" It was very late, and for some reason the heat in the building was fucked up, and the room was freezing cold. We sat on the floor, like always, and the candle was flickering and sputtering very low. I think it has only about an hour of burning time left in it. So we sat there, and I kept thinking about my Intellectual History class I'd have to wake up at ten for the next morning, and I started wishing the whole meeting was over and done with and that I could just go to sleep, like a normal person. There was no spark at all to the session. Finally Laura started reading from Sexton's Transformations. It was really fine, but I didn't have it in me to listen, and I think Laura could tell. We ended very early. When I woke up this morning I actually felt rested—something I haven't felt in a long time. It was wonderful; I didn't even have to take a nap this afternoon.

Don't worry about anyone finding out where you are, I'm not telling. And yes, I do think you should inform the registrar.

If you don't, they'll think something happened to you and will call Security to open your door with a master key, and everyone will crowd around in the hall, expecting to see you dangling from the rafters . . .

Seriously, though, please take care of yourself out there. I know you explained the situation very plainly in your letter, and it all sounded kosher, but I think that something eventually has to give. Write me immediately.

Love,
Naomi

Dear Dear Claire,

Oh, tell me already! The three of you are getting a great big kick out of this whole thing, aren't you? In order to get this letter to you, I have to go through complicated channels. I've been instructed to meet Naomi and Laura in front of the library at noon on Wednesday. They'll put the address on the envelope after I walk away—I only have to put on a stamp. I'm suspicious of them steaming the letter open and giggling over it—it all makes me sick. So in order not to make a fool of myself I'm keeping this letter short and sane. Only know that underneath these words is my concern for you and, despite myself, my love. Please, Claire.

Julian

Dearest Claire,

Your father and I had a long talk the other day after we got your letter. In fact, as you can probably guess, we have not stopped talking about the whole matter. I wasn't going to write to you, but I changed my mind. After all, I am your mother, and I should let you know my feelings. You are a young woman now and are getting too old for this kind of rebellion. When you were in high school we just ignored you, because things were difficult around the house and your guidance counselor said you would grow out of it soon enough. I'm finding it hard to just keep ignoring it now. No, I'm not going to force you to come home or anything like that. You are an adult in many ways. I just think you should be aware of the other factors involved. That college of yours is not cheap, even with the financial-aid package you are getting. But the money is going to be taken away from you in a jiffy as soon as the financial-aid office gets wind of what you are doing. They will give your money to someone who deserves it more, someone who knows enough to stay in school for the semester. If you were having personal problems you should have gone to see the school psychologist. Your father and I would not have objected to that. I don't really understand what you are getting out of living in these people's home. You always carried things too far, even when you were little. All three of you kids were like that. I have never understood your fascination for this poetess, and I guess I never will. I'm trying to keep an open mind about this, but I have to say that I think something has gone wrong. When the Kahns' son Bobby overdosed on heroin a few years ago and had to go to Phoenix House, I knew it had to do with the parents, who were always fighting and throwing things and the neighbors complained all the time. He was a troubled boy and yes his parents made him that way. I know life has not been easy since Seth passed away, but I think we have tried our hardest to remain a family. Incidentally, your sister Joan called to tell us that she is getting married. The wedding is planned for the spring, and her fiancé is someone named Steven Blackwing who is an Indian as you can guess from his name. Your father and I cannot decide whether or not we will go to the wedding. Airfare is so expensive, and we know nothing about this man, except that he makes turquoise jewelry for a living and that he and Joan plan on staying on the reservation after they get married. Your sister's chore is to bring fresh water to the Indians in buckets each day. How's that for a job. Needless to say, we are not thrilled, and right now I feel under a lot of stress. It's not that I stay up nights worrying about you. I trust that you are being well fed and that these are decent people, since that's what you told me. But I think you should take a good, hard look at your life and try to figure out what is really best. I am getting too old to check up on my children all the time. The time has come for me to start enjoying my life. Tonight your father and I are going to see Dionne Warwick at the Westbury Music Fair, and I am looking forward to it. It's theater-in-the-round, so all of the seats are good. I'm going to end this letter now and start to make dinner. I have nothing more to add, except that I hope you will think about what I have said.

Love,
Mother

Dear Claire,

What do you mean by "I feel as though the ghost of Lucy Ascher is wandering through the rooms of the house"? Do you seriously mean that, or are you just being your usual metaphorical self? Don't tell me you've started to believe in the supernatural. I don't think I could take it. One of the things I've always liked best about you is your straightforward, no-shit view of the world, and I couldn't stand it if you came back to school brandishing a deck of tarot cards and sounding like that woman Sybil Leek, who claims she's a witch.

From the way you described it, I do *think your mother's response was totally weird and uncalled for, but I have to tell you, if we're going to keep things honest and open, that I'm getting a little worried about you being out there, and I think that maybe you* should *consider coming home one of these days. I hope you won't hate me forever for saying that. Your mother sounds as though she's really angry with you for letting her down or something, but I think she's worried, too. I wish you would hurry and purge yourself at the Aschers' and then come back to school. I'll take you out for a big reunion dinner—lobster tails and Baskin-Robbins, your favorites.*

You know me, always worrying about everyone else. Remember last year I typed up Laura's entire English paper— seventeen pages, with two pages worth of footnotes—because she was really overworked and I thought she would collapse if she had to stay up and type, and then I ended up getting a mediocre grade on my French final because I didn't get a chance to study for it. So there you are. I'm worried about

Laura once again, and I wanted to ask your advice, if you have any to give. I think I wrote you about her in my last letter—about how she spent the evening out in the snow (or said she did) and then acted really weird and depressed when we went inside. Anyway, things have only gotten worse since then. I don't understand it; I can't see that anything has happened in her life recently to affect her this way. The other day when I asked her what was up, she just closed her eyes and said in this sarcastic voice, "The human condition." She hasn't been going to her classes lately. She has this really intensive seminar with Miller—you know the one—and last week she seemed to be really excited about it. They're reading The Magic Mountain *now, which has always been one of her favorite books. You know, all that heavy Germanic lust and angst. The other day I walked by her classroom and saw that she wasn't there, so I went back to her dorm and she was lying in bed with her clothes on, the same ones she had worn the day before, and she seemed really out of it. I asked her if she'd forgotten about her class, and she didn't even know what I was talking about. It took her about five minutes to orient herself. I asked her what was wrong, and she wouldn't tell me. She said she didn't think she could trust me anymore, and I have to admit I was pretty hurt by that. You know how close we've been. At any rate, I asked her how she felt about talking to the school shrink, and she shrugged and said it didn't matter to her, so I called up and made an appointment for Friday. I just hope she'll go. If she keeps acting this way do you think I should press the issue, or just leave her alone until she feels like confiding in me?*

It is now almost nine o'clock at night and I haven't done a damn thing work-wise this evening. I have to finish up this letter and then get over to the library, where tons of glorious reserve reading are just waiting to be devoured. Please come home when you're ready to, which I hope is soon. I know that part of this feeling is selfishness (I'm lonely!) but most of it is worry. God, what do you do all day other than clean out their toilet bowl and change their sheets? Do they know your real reason for being there yet?

Listen, it only took me a single afternoon to get my entire Plath fill, so why should it take you so long to get your fill of Lucy Ascher? Don't be greedy. Just think of all the other "death girls," to coin a Swarthmore phrase, absolutely dying to sneak their way into the Aschers' house and poke around. Come back to school and give someone else a chance. I miss you, Laura misses you, and Julian misses you. He looks like a lost dog without you, Claire. I told him for about the millionth time you were fine, which I hope is the truth. You know, I'm actually starting to find him a little appealing. So get out of that house as soon as you can, before that ghost goes to your head. And in the meantime, take care of yourself.

Love,
Naomi

Oh Claire,

Why haven't I heard from you? Please write to me now. I rush to my mailbox each morning, hoping to see the darkness of a letter waiting inside. I can just picture it—on that really thin, delicate stationery scented with that whale-sperm perfume you use. You know just what gets me, don't you?

I have to let you know that I miss you more than you can ever imagine. I never thought I could feel this way about anyone. When I was seeing that girl Cathy back in my Dalton days, I was positive I really loved her and that that was the extent of what love could be. As I'm writing this, I realize how stupid it sounds, but I guess I must be a stupid person. The thing about Cathy that attracted me to her was how delicate she was. We used to walk through the halls in school (we were like this famous couple, and all the teachers would smile at us), and I would always have my arm around her. One day I realized I was doing this not so much because I wanted to touch her, but because I wanted to protect her. Sometimes if we went outside and it started to drizzle, I would put my hand over her head without even thinking about it. She was like this little bud or something that I wanted to take care of. I figured out that that was the only reason why I liked being with her so much, and it really upset me. We broke up a couple of weeks later. What's different about you is that I know you don't need anyone to protect you from the world. I think you need someone to protect you from yourself.

This letter, which I wanted to be meaningful, is turning out to be loaded with clichés. I can't help it; I have a tendency to take the easy way out, to say, "Oh, you know how I feel," instead of actually saying how it is I feel. I don't know why this whole thing happened between us—I mean our relationship to begin with—and the more I think about it, the more I realize it probably shouldn't have happened at all. I love you to an extent that is making me feel really awful. You haven't exactly been generous with yourself. I almost never know what you're thinking—not just about me, but about everything. There was one time that you made me feel great, I don't know if you remember it. We were lying in bed at night, and you turned to me and said, "Julian, you're a good person." And then you went to sleep.

That was one of the rare moments we've had. I usually have to guess what you're thinking, and I end up feeling dumb. I must have no pride whatsoever that I put up with your coldness, with your hanging up on me that night. I keep thinking about our conversation, trying to understand what it was I said to make you angry or upset, or whatever it was you were feeling. Was it my joke about how you taste good? I can't believe it was. I've made so many hokey jokes in the past, and you haven't seemed to mind. Maybe your anger has been building up and that joke was the last straw. Or did it only have to do with Lucy Ascher? You got so resistant when I brought up that book. It's as if she's private property that only you're allowed to touch. I think if I understand her, then I can begin to understand you. Does that scare you? Are you afraid that if I take away the mysterious part of you, I won't like you anymore?

It's exhausting not to understand you, to have to spend my nights trying to figure you out. Yes, you have ruined my college life, in case you were wondering. I've started to spend all my time with Lenny Garibaldi, etc.—"the boys," as you say. We get very stoned and we listen to old Dylan, and then I go off into a little dream world about you. I can't sleep well anymore.

My parents are concerned about me. They call up twice a week and tell me to take things easy. They want me to spend a weekend with them somewhere in the country. I keep telling them no, because I'm afraid I'll start getting teary in the car, and they'll think I'm having some kind of trauma, which I am.

The other day Naomi came up to me when I was sitting in the Student Union and she said, "Cheer up, Julian." I couldn't believe it was her. She's always been so nasty to me in the past. I guess I must look out of it, which is the way I feel. I had no idea it showed so much. As I write this letter, I realize it's going to end up being the longest one I've ever written. So instead of doing my real work, I'm doing this. I hope it's worth something.

I guess it's pretty obvious that I'm not exactly the most experienced person in the world. I mean, I've had other girl-friends before you, and even other extended romances. It's just that things were simpler then. I could bring a single rose to Cathy and she would think it was the most beautiful, original thought in the world. When we had sex for the first time, I had to swear I wouldn't hurt her. I didn't even know what that meant; I knew nothing about sex or about hurting any-one. I was just this excited kid, and I agreed to anything. I didn't know what I was doing.

But now I think I do. When I was with you, I felt very overwhelmed, but I also felt as if I knew what was going on. I knew that when we slept together it wasn't as good as it could

*or should have been. I was aware of that from the start.
Sexual problems aren't supposed to creep up until we're in our
forties—I'm supposed to become impotent then, and you're
supposed to have a headache all the time. Then we go to a
marriage counselor and work everything out, and the sex
becomes great again. But I'm only twenty, and you're not
even. What are we doing wrong? The more I think about it,
the more I think we're doing nothing wrong—it's just the
nature of our relationship. Somewhere in this letter I mentioned how we shouldn't have gotten together in the first place.
Maybe that's why sex is so difficult. I can't come up with any
other reason. The first time you took off your turtleneck, and
all that static made your hair fly out, I had this huge smile
on my face—I don't know if you saw. I was so wrapped up
in watching you, I didn't know what to do with myself.
Claire, you have such a beautiful body. Why do you hide it
in black all the time?*

*You're so secretive about your history—have other people
gone crazy over you before? Are you used to this kind of letter?
You never told me anything about other boys/men in your past,
and while I was very curious, I didn't want to push. I'm always
afraid something I say will alienate you, and sure enough,
something did. I keep telling myself I have to be careful when
dealing with you, but I don't even know what that entails. It's
like walking across a mine field. Trial and error. If you could
just give me an idea of what I can and can't say, then things
would be better between us. Incomplete, probably, but better,
because I wouldn't feel so tense whenever I said anything that
was important to me, wondering if you would shut me out.*

What goes on inside of you? Do you have some deep dark secret that you're trying to hide? After spending so much time with "the boys," I've started thinking of things in terms of TV trivia. This whole thing reminds me of an episode of Medical Center, *in which this guy is deaf, and Chad Everett thinks it's a case of hysterical deafness. He thinks something terrible happened to the guy when he was a kid and that he's been repressing it all these years. He wants to explore the guy's past to get at the heart of what he's been repressing, but the family won't let him. They start to take the guy out of the hospital, and as they're wheeling him from the room, Chad Everett has to think fast, so he knocks over a huge tray of glasses. The guy, who's already halfway out the door and his back is turned, jumps at the crash. The family realizes that deep inside, the guy really can hear, so they agree to let him stay for more tests. It ends with this flashback to when the guy was little and his father beat him up or something. When he remembers it, he can suddenly hear again. It was a stupid show, but pretty cool in a way. Maybe you have something like that that makes you so secretive and closed, something you want to hide. It's just a thought.*

I've been sitting here at my desk for hours and it's just occurred to me how tired I am. I have a stiff neck from lean-ing over too long. Before I go to bed to dream about you, I'd like to make a request. Please tell me where you are. I prom-ise I won't do anything to embarrass you—I just want to know. It would give me a better perspective on the whole situation. If you are out with some man in the wilderness, eating grape nuts and having a wonderful, back to nature

*time and you tell me that the two of you are very much in
love, then I'll bow out as gracefully as I can. I want to know
if I have a chance with you anymore and if you ever think
about me. I hate to be repetitive, but I think this letter is going
to end the same way my last one did: Please, Claire.*

Julian

She sat on the bed with the pile of letters on her lap. All her
life she had wished for mail—for anything, even a chain letter.
She had always been the first one out the door at home when
she heard the postman coming up the walk. There was hardly
ever anything for her, but still she remained hopeful. At summer camp when the mail bell clanged she would race from her
bunk. Her parents sent infrequent, chatty notes telling her
what movies they had gone to see, whose barbecues they had
been to, how the parakeet was doing. Claire could never get
enough of those letters; they made her feel connected to something.

And now, just when she wanted it least, she received mail
almost every day. "Here's another one for you," Helen would
say, handing her an envelope. Naomi, Julian, her mother—
three people who were concerned about her. Their letters were
small reminders of her life outside the Aschers' house, and she
didn't want to be reminded. Claire could not be angry with
them, though; they meant well.

One thing in Naomi's first letter had intrigued her. Did
people at Swarthmore really think something might have happened to her since she left school? Did she come across as

suicidal? It was strange; Claire had never given any serious thought to taking her own life. There were times when she fantasized about it, of course, but she knew she would never carry it through. In all her fantasies, she imagined herself being saved. She pictured herself waking up in a hospital bed, with a young woman psychiatrist peering down at her. Claire would spend a few weeks in the hospital, and she and the doctor would iron out all of her problems and become close friends. She would leave the place feeling refreshed, rejuvenated.

This wasn't a death wish, Claire knew. She still held on to the frayed ends of life, and always would. That was what separated her from Lucy. It was not a matter of courage, of having the guts to complete the act. Like Lucy, Claire felt the darkness all around her, but unlike Lucy, she had no idea of what it meant to walk through that darkness, to move beyond it. Certain things pulled her back. She looked down at the pile of letters and wondered which of them she should answer first.

chapter ten

Claire was polishing the silverware. She was sitting alone at the kitchen table, rubbing each piece with silver paste and a soft felt cloth. Her hands were dark with tarnish. She seemed occupied, really occupied, as if she were doing something of an intellectual nature. She squinted to clean out the tiny rosette grooves that were notched into each handle. A wedding gift long ago, from Ray's parents. The Aschers used it as both their everyday and their special-occasion silver. And now Claire was polishing it carefully, as though it would really matter—as though, when Helen held up a teaspoon now, her inverted reflection, clear as day for the first time in years, would change anything.

Helen went upstairs to the bedroom and sprawled out on the unmade bed. Lying there, the shades still pulled all the way down, she was reminded of the early days after the death, when she never knew what time it was, because the room stayed dark. Once Harriet Crane, wife of a dean, marched in and snapped open the window shade. The shade flew up on its roller, the light flooded in. "Come on, Helen," Harriet said in a brisk voice, but then she faltered as she got a good look at Helen lying there in the stale room. "I'm sorry," Harriet said, quickly pulling the shade back down and hurrying out.

Now Helen went and opened the shades herself. It was a mild morning, and cloudless. She began to make the bed; she didn't want to wait until Claire got around to doing it. The sight of an unmade bed always gave her a sick feeling. She bent over and smoothed down the floral sheets, and that was when the telephone rang. It was a jarring sound to her because it was so infrequent. She reached across the bed and answered it. "Hello," she said.

It was a woman, and her voice came on quickly. "Mrs. Ascher," she said. "I want to speak to Mrs. Ascher."

"Speaking," said Helen.

There was a wait. "Look," said the woman, "I'll get right to the point. It's about my daughter."

There had been a few calls like this before—parents saying that their daughters were depressed, were spending too much time alone in their rooms, were acting strange, were maybe suicidal. What should they do about it?

"I'm sorry," Helen said. "I really can't help you."

"Please," the woman said. "Just listen to me. I know my daughter is there. She told me herself. Please don't pretend."

Claire's mother. The realization occurred to Helen all at once. "Mrs. Danziger," she said. "I wasn't thinking. I'm sorry."

"I don't know what kind of a person you are," said Claire's mother, "but this whole thing is very troubling to my husband and me. Claire was a Dean's List student every semester, you know. I told her we wouldn't interfere, but I'm finding it very hard to just sit back and let this continue."

Downstairs Claire was working, her shoes kicked off, at ease in this new house. What was her family life like? The voice of her mother was tight and strained. Am I a child stealer, Helen wondered—one of those pathetic women who pluck toddlers from their strollers? It had never occurred to her that Claire might really belong somewhere else and actually be missed. At once she saw that this had been a stupid oversight on her part.

"Mrs. Danziger," she said, "I never imagined that this would cause any difficulties. I'd assumed Claire was, well, on her own, making decisions for herself. She never gave us a clue . . . If I had known this would have caused so many problems, I certainly wouldn't have hired her. I hope you understand."

The woman's voice relaxed a little. "I was just worried," she said, "when Claire told us she was doing this. It sounded so irrational, but she's always been headstrong. What could I do?"

"Kids are that way," Helen found herself saying, feeling as though this were slowly leading into a neighborly conversation— two women chatting over the backyard fence, laundry flapping in the afternoon breeze. Had she ever had a conversation like that before? She vaguely remembered a chat with another woman about how hard it was to be a parent in this day and age.

Helen had attended a PTA meeting once. Newsletters and invitations kept arriving in the mail, and she finally went, purely out of guilt. She sat in the back row of the dark auditorium while a panel on stage discussed drug abuse in the community.

"So remember," the moderator said. "If you child starts staying out late, or asking for his allowance early, or spending time with children who are not familiar to you, be alert. And also watch out for the sweet, ropy odor of marijuana . . . "

Helen drifted off. What was a ropy odor? Did rope really have a smell of its own? She became light-headed sitting there, stuffed into a wool dress she had bought years earlier for a nephew's graduation from Cornell. There was nothing of relevance being said at the meeting. Lucy never went out in the evenings and never asked for money. On Fridays after school Ray gave her her allowance and she took it from him silently, usually spending it on used books of poetry—Roethke, Stevens, Lowell.

"You know, I took a poetry class when I was at Hunter," Helen had said to Lucy once. Lucy waited for her to go on, to elaborate, but Helen could not think of anything else to say. She couldn't even think of the names of any of the poems she had read. Abbey, Lines Written over something Abbey. A half-title rose and fell in her mind. She was sorry she had brought up the subject; she hadn't liked the class and had not been a very good student. The professor was a snide man who used his students' names like weapons. "Well, Miss *Hertz*," he would say when asking a question, leaning over and closing in for the kill. He did not like women, Helen had heard; maybe he just did not like people in general. She had been relieved to retreat to the safety of the Chemistry lab when English ended each morning.

Kids are that way, Helen said to Claire's mother, as though she had been saying it for years, commiserating with other mothers, sniffing gleefully around the house for that elusive ropy odor.

"Do you want to speak to Claire?" Helen asked. "She's just downstairs."

The woman hesitated. "No," she said. "Not yet, not today. She would just resent me more. Please don't tell her that I called. She wants a first taste of independence, she can have it. I guess that means cutting the apron strings, as they say."

"Yes," said Helen. "I guess it does. I've been through that."

There was a pause. "Your daughter—your Lucy," said Mrs. Danziger. "I think Claire could practically teach a course on her poetry, she knows it so well."

Helen did not say anything. She felt blood rush to her head. She was always thrown off balance when she heard anyone else mention Lucy. Even the name was tragic—the two simple syllables, the name you would give to a pretty little baby.

"I'm sorry," said Claire's mother. "I should have been quiet. I mean, I don't even know if this is something you talk about with other people. I know how it is."

"You know how it is?" Helen asked. She didn't mean it nastily; she was just curious.

"Yes," the woman said in a new, soft voice. "We lost our child too."

There was something moving over the line then; both women let out a small sound of relief. All the lost children, Helen thought, and her head filled with images. She thought of that passage in Lucy's journal in which she wrote about being lost in a department store. Helen took this further; she imagined the whole world as a gigantic department store, and you could claim your lost child at the information desk. She would run through the crowd of shoppers, knocking over mannequins as she ran, and scoop up lost Lucy in her arms.

"I didn't know that," Helen said, awkward. "Claire never told us."

"She doesn't talk about it much," said Mrs. Danziger. "She's been very quiet about it. They were very close. They had a lot of private jokes. You wouldn't think it, but Claire used to laugh at things with Seth. They used to tell knock-knock jokes over dinner . . . " Her voice trailed off in the middle of the sentence, and she said, "I really don't know why I'm telling you all this. I called up to insist that Claire come home, that I'd had enough of her games, but now I guess I'm just running off at the mouth."

"It's all right," said Helen. "Please. You just get wrapped up in a thought and start talking. Everybody does that sometimes."

"True," said Mrs. Danziger.

"It's like therapy—they say it's good to talk," Helen said. "Most of the time it's hard for me."

"My husband and I, we've tried to focus on other things," said Claire's mother. "He's joined a gym now. Twice a week he goes with other men from work. It's co-ed, 'unisex,' they call it, but I'd be embarrassed to go and have to show everybody how out of shape I am. I'll find something else to do. You have to keep busy; that's all there is."

Keep busy. People had said this to Helen before. She

imagined herself running around, trying to find new hobbies—learning to knit, perhaps, and knitting so rapidly that the needles clicked like a field of crickets. Or she could take up Evelyn Wood, the pages of all the classics flipping by in a great fan. But what was the rush, anyway? We are here for quite a while, she thought. If she and Ray sped through everything, they would eventually have nothing left. They would have to turn to each other then, and they would probably be like two aging virgins, two people alone and hesitant in a room, mouths waiting to press, buttons waiting to be sprung.

Helen had gone to the Brooklyn Public Library at eighteen and read everything she could find on sex. *Libido. Multiple Orgasms.* It was comforting to apply clinical terms to those feelings, to the way everything inside seemed to rise to the surface when Ray touched her—the flush of blood to her face, the little pebbles that rose to her nipples. All that was gone now.

The only thing that parents of lost children could do was turn to one another, as if in a huge square dance when you look your partner, a stranger, dead in the eye and cross your arms for a do-si-do, barely touching as you move to the music.

"Mrs. Danziger," said Helen, "Claire will be all right. I'll make sure of it; I promise you."

"I just hope she can straighten herself out," said Mrs. Danziger. "She hangs around with such odd girls at college, and she has some boyfriend who we've never met, but I'm sure he's no better. I've been worrying about her for ages, and now all this."

"Things need time," Helen said.

"Time," Claire's mother echoed. "I know."

The conversation did not really end; it just dissolved in the air. Each woman was moving further into herself, into her old grief. After Helen hung up the telephone she sat for a while longer on the bed. There had been something between the two of them. Downstairs was a child who did not belong to Helen and Ray, someone they were merely borrowing for a short time.

She told Ray late that night when they were undressing for bed. He slipped out of his boxer shorts and into a pair of creased cotton pajama bottoms. He sat up and breathed in his stomach, something she had noticed him doing a lot lately. She did not mention it. "I got an interesting phone call today," she said.

"A weird one, you mean?"

"Not exactly. Claire's mother."

He raised his eyebrows. "What did she want?" he asked.

"I'm not altogether sure," said Helen. "At first she was practically accusing us of kidnapping Claire, but then I think she realized that wasn't what was going on. She talked to me about things. They had a child who died, you know."

"So there's more to Claire," Ray said, bringing his feet up onto the bed and reaching to shut off the light.

Helen was feeling very talkative that night. She placed her hand gently over his, so he wouldn't switch off the lamp. "Keep it on," she said. "I don't think I could sleep just yet. I feel all wired up."

"About Claire?" he asked.

"Yes," she said. "I've kind of latched on to this fact, about her parents having had another child, and Claire being the survivor and all that."

"She doesn't look too much like a survivor," Ray said.

Helen had to agree that that was true. "Most of us don't," she added.

"Well, most of us have good reasons," said Ray.

This was their old banter now. It was odd how easily they could drop back into it. People living together developed patterns that held forever, it seemed.

Claire was asleep already. Ray said her light had been off when he passed her room. She had worked steadily all day, then gone upstairs to bed. At dinner she had eaten very little—a plate of soup, some broccoli, a glass of milk. "Some chicken?" Helen had asked, the platter poised in the air.

"No thank you," Claire said. "I've decided not to eat meat for a few days."

Lucy had had vegetarian leanings, too. Every few months, though, she would claim to need a steak, and so Helen and Ray would gladly take her out to a noisy, dark steakhouse. She ate her meat rare, digging into a thick London broil expertly. When she was done she would pat her mouth lightly with a napkin, and they would leave the restaurant. It was as though she had to be refueled every so often and would run for months at a time powered by the protein of one steak dinner.

Claire ate like a bird. Helen wondered if she, too, had sudden cravings for red meat. Helen liked the delicate way Claire spooned up soup. Everything about her manner was careful, guarded. She sat straight in her chair, eating small mouthfuls, and swallowing milk silently. She was well-contained, this child.

When dinner ended, Claire stood and began to clear the

table. Ray went into the den to grade papers, and Helen stayed in her chair. As Claire worked, there was the sound of silver being piled—a shuffle of metal. The knives and forks glinted with a new light that evening; Claire had polished them well. Now she ran warm water over each piece and placed it in the dishwasher rack. Helen wasn't needed in the kitchen, but she stayed anyway. She liked watching and listening; it lulled her. Claire handled things gently. Underneath all that hardness she was someone's sister, lover, daughter.

chapter eleven

The ghost of Lucy Ascher would not go away. Claire did not want it to, but that was hardly the point. As the days passed she realized that Lucy, in her subtle way, managed to be everywhere. The house reeked of her presence. Since no one mentioned it, Claire wondered if perhaps she was the only one who was aware of this phenomenon, the only one who felt that Lucy was still very much a part of the household.

Ray and Helen barely spoke about their daughter, and when they did, it was in a quiet, off-hand manner. One night at dinner Helen murmured something about wanting to get rid of some boxes of old clothes that were taking up space in the garage.

"They were our daughter's," Ray said quietly to Claire.

"Oh," she responded, looking down into her bowl of soup. "I see."

After a few moments of the silence that accompanied most meals at the Aschers', Claire offered in as casual a voice as she could muster to take care of the clothing. Helen Ascher waved her hand in careless agreement. Ray told her he thought it was a fine idea.

The next morning, her eighth day with the Aschers, she put on her coat and went out to the garage, which was separate from the house. The place smelled good; Claire had always loved the mingled odors of exhaust and gasoline. Whenever her parents drove to a gas station, Claire would roll down her window all the way and inhale the fumes. "Sicko," her mother would call her whenever she did this.

The garage was truly a mess, unlike the house, which had a kind of shabby order to it. There were beach chairs with split canvas seats scattered around. In a corner was a coffee table whose surface someone had begun to finish and then had obviously abandoned. The partially shellacked table was surrounded by newspaper and hardened brushes crusted with lacquer. On the walls were garden tools hanging on hooks: a spade, a trowel, a rake with a cracked handle. Claire wondered why they were there, since there was obviously no garden to tend. Nothing grew in a bed of sand, or if it did, it would certainly have to choke its own way up into open sunlight without the aid of water.

There were old, bad oil paintings propped against the wall. There was an antique globe resting on its axis. Claire picked it up and spun it slowly. She saw that all of the countries and oceans and islands were written in German. *Frankreich*, she read. *Atlantischer Ozean*. There was a Miss Clairol electric hair curler set piled on top of a precarious stack of matching books. Claire moved the curlers and picked up the first book. *Ocean- ography Abstracts* it read on the spine, *Vol. XII, 1962*. The book felt damp and furred, as though a strain of bread mold had grown on its cover. She dropped it back onto the pile, and a small cloud of dust billowed up.

The entire garage was like this, a roomful of useless, sense- less things just waiting to disintegrate over the course of time. She was freezing, and she was about to turn and leave when she remembered what she had gone there for in the first place. The boxes of clothing.

She found them easily enough; they were behind a folded card table, three cartons, all of them labeled "Lucy." She dragged them out to the center of the floor, where there was a little square of cleared space. She opened the first box with trembling, cold hands. Inside was darkness, but the box was not empty. It was stuffed to the top with Lucy's black and gray and navy-blue sweaters and dresses and shirts. Claire felt a sudden kinship, greater than she had ever felt before. She pulled out a turtleneck, ribbed and black, and held it up against her own chest and arms. The ghost of Lucy Ascher hovered overhead, smiling.

I t was Ray who went to look for her, hours later. He came into the garage to see how she was making out, and he stopped in the doorway. She was modeling a dress, Lucy's dress, before an imaginary mirror, holding it out in a fan shape at the sides. When she saw him she dropped her hands, embar- rassed.

The dress was not a perfect fit—Lucy had been somewhat smaller than Claire—but it hung fairly well nonetheless. It was made of black crepe, and the material was creased into long, soft folds. Claire smoothed it down against her and looked up at Ray.

"You know about Lucy," he said.

"Yes." She could not have said anything else and gotten away with it. Naomi had been right, her face betrayed her. It wasn't her mouth, it was her eyes. They widened, darkened. She had been wearing the clothes of Lucy Ascher, after all. She had trembled almost violently as she drew the dress over her head. She had taken off her own clothes, her jeans and turtleneck, in the freezing garage. Her skin had risen into gooseflesh from the excitement and from the cold. Her nipples stood out in hard, tight points. She could smell the scent of Lucy on the dress—something pungent and sad and wise. She wondered if later, when she took the dress off and put her own clothes back on, that smell would remain on her skin. She hoped it would.

Ray stood watching her from the doorway. He was wearing a cap with earflaps on it. She looked at him and she did not know what to say. He didn't move, he just kept watching. "Are you angry?" she asked finally, for she could not tell what he was thinking.

"No," he said. "Why should I be angry?"

"I don't know," Claire said. "I thought you'd think it was disrespectful of me."

He shook his head slowly. "No, I don't think that. I was surprised, that's all. It really didn't have too much to do with you."

"What did it have to do with?" she asked, curious.

Ray sat down on the step that led into the garage. He crossed his arms over his chest and thought about it. "You looked like her," he said softly. "Like Lucy, when she used to wear that dress. It startled me, that's all."

There were long pauses between each of their sentences. The conversation seemed suspended in the cold air. When either of them spoke, vapor came out first. It was a very uncomfortable talk. Claire tried to make herself appear relaxed. She leaned against the wall, her hand draped over a bicycle tire that hung there. She knew how stilted and oddly formal she must look. God, she was wearing a party dress, a dress that had been worn to receptions, to poetry readings, a dress that had absorbed the benign sweat of Lucy Ascher as she cleared her throat into a microphone behind some podium.

If there was ever a time to make a confession, this was it. "Listen," Claire said at last. "I have something to tell you. I didn't come here randomly. I knew what I was doing."

She sought for more words, but he interrupted her. "You don't have to say anything," he said. "It doesn't really matter why you're here, does it? Helen said it didn't."

It was the most awkward conversation Claire had ever had. She was choosing her words very carefully. "Helen knows?" she asked. "Knows that I know?"

"We've talked about you," he admitted. "But we've never really said much. We've just mentioned you. I've wanted to say more to Helen, but . . . things are hard for her."

Ray was looking at Claire more intently now, and it

unnerved her. "Maybe I should leave," she said. "I don't know how good an idea this is."

"No," he said. "Why should you? Things will be okay here." Then, as if on impulse, he said, "Tell me about yourself."

"There's nothing to tell," Claire answered quickly. "I just wanted to come here. I thought it would be a good experience." She hated herself at once for minimizing her love for Lucy, but there was nothing else she could do. Her heart was beating rapidly, and she played her feelings down. "That's about all," she said, then she shrugged and tried to smile.

They left it at that. She could not say anything more, and soon he stood up and walked back to the house. "You should come inside too," he called over his shoulder. "It's a lot warmer."

And so they had an unspoken relationship from then on. Ray still shuffled into the kitchen each morning for breakfast while she stood unloading the dishwasher. They exchanged the required hellos and nothing more. Everything that mattered was left unsaid. Claire didn't think of this silence as mutual indifference; she thought of it as a kind of tacit communication. She was aware that Ray regarded her with interest now. One Sunday she was cooking breakfast for them, and when she handed him his plate of eggs, sunny side up and crisp around the edges, he looked up at her, eyes full of feeling, and said, "These are just perfect, Claire."

Still the ghost was everywhere, its presence amplified by the fact that nobody ever mentioned it. How did that perfume commercial go—something like "If you want to catch someone's attention, whisper." Claire thought that this might well be true. She had just begun to realize that subtleties were everything. In bed at night at the Aschers', she would feel the soft whoosh of fingers down her back, the slightest hint of breath, and it would be more than enough to carry her through the night. Claire certainly had not lived her life by this doctrine. She knew that everything she did was overboard—the way she dressed, or wore perfume, or carried an obsession to the hilt. She had never thought of subtlety as being effective. She needed immediate response, immediate gratification. People turned their heads and watched when she came into a classroom. Claire needed that rush of recognition; it let her know that she was still alive, still breathing. Without it, she feared she might fade into anonymity, into a walking death.

What was it, then, that made her a death girl? She certainly didn't embrace death. In fact, she was very much frightened by it. Maybe it was this fear that had stunned her into a kind of obsessiveness. If you put yourself in a perpetual state of mourning, then nothing could come up from behind and surprise you. You were prepared for everything—telegrams, landslides, avalanches, apocalypse. When Seth died Claire had thought, I can't go through this again. She knew she would have to, though. She knew that it was usual for children eventually to bury their parents. Chances were that she would not have to think about this for a couple of decades, and when she did she would not be alone; she would be flanked by other people—a husband and children. The way society worked, you replaced your family with a new one—a young, rock-strong husband and a newborn infant—so that when your first family gave way, there would be a buffer to the blow. You would hardly feel it;

you would only sense something inside, a slight vibration of change, like a tuning fork being struck against a table edge. There would be new people standing on either side of you in the cemetery, holding an umbrella over your head, steadying you with their arms.

Some people were unlucky; they lived to see everything. When all of the relatives came back to the Danzigers' house after Seth's funeral, Claire made herself useful, carrying plates of food back and forth. On a trip into the kitchen she found her grandmother sitting at the table in one of the swivel chairs, moving it slowly from side to side. "Claire," the woman said, "no grandmother should ever have to see this."

What kind of sense could you make of death when you grew old? What could you make of the ritual of mourning? The mirrors in the house had all been draped with sheets. They looked like flattened ghosts or paintings about to be unveiled at an exhibition. Claire had asked Rabbi Krinsky what the significance of covering the mirrors was. He told her that she had asked a very important question and explained to her that the mirrors were covered so that there should be no vanity. Claire had nodded, moving away from him. The custom made perfect sense to her, and probably even more to her grandmother. There had to be *something* to keep you forging ahead in times of grief—some feeling of self. Of course the mirrors were covered. It might be tempting, she thought, to glance up in the mirror if it was left bare and catch a piece of your reflection for one brief moment, feeling a sudden rush of guilty pride, the vanity of just being alive.

To be a bereaved grandmother was terrible, a freak of

nature, but to be a bereaved parent was even worse. Claire realized, with a little surprise, that her parents and the Aschers actually had something in common. It had never occurred to her before. The resemblance was confined to the fact that each couple had lost a child; it went no further than that. Grief had made her parents hard, and it had softened the Aschers.

What bewilderment the Aschers must be feeling in the middle of all that grief. After all, Lucy's death was a kind of unsolved mystery. Her whole essence was a mystery, the eighth wonder of the world. Claire no longer knew how people's personalities are shaped. Genetics could not begin to explain it; the twisted double helix of DNA didn't have enough room to hold codes for despair or anger or alienation. Those traits were learned, and Lucy didn't seem to have learned them from her parents. Helen and Ray had been happy once and hopeful about their world.

Maybe you have to give children more credit than that, Claire thought. Maybe they absorbed larger things, were sensitive to a woman crying in the street, an argument on television, the way light slants in through a window at a certain time of day.

Perhaps the Aschers just weren't the right parents for Lucy. They were good people; they just weren't right for their daughter. Lucy needed something else, but what? Claire didn't know, and she never would. She realized then that she wouldn't be able to find out too much about Lucy by living in the Aschers' house. If someone moved into the Danzigers' house now in the hope of learning about Claire, what would she find? Clues, but some of them would be red herrings. There was an Anne Sexton line that Laura often repeated—something about how every woman is her mother. Claire didn't think she believed that; it was too easy, too pat. You have to take what you are given and then use it to move forward. You can't remain static all your life.

There had been the slightest change in Helen lately, Claire noticed. She wondered if Ray had said anything to his wife after the conversation in the garage. Helen still had the same glazed expression on her face, and her eyes still moved as though she were watching a "follow the bouncing ball" cartoon, but every once in a while Claire could see a hint of recognition coming through. The first time she noticed it was one evening when she came downstairs to have dinner. Helen and Ray were already seated at the table, and as Claire came into the kitchen, Helen looked up at her and held her gaze. It startled Claire, but she tried not to show it. She sat in her chair as though she had not seen the change.

After dinner Ray pulled her aside in the kitchen alcove. Helen was washing pots. The water was rushing loudly, and she could not hear their talk. "You know, she seems happier tonight," he said. "Don't you think?"

She looked at him and saw that he was desperate. He was confiding in her only because he needed to talk and she was there. "Yes," Claire said. "She does."

Her confirmation of this seemed to put him in good spirits, and later that evening when the dishwasher had been put on and the three of them were sitting quietly in the living room, Ray said to Claire, "I want to show you something." Helen looked up from the beach-grass place mat she was working on, inquisitive. "The telescope," he explained to his wife.

"Oh," she said, her eyes bright for a moment, and then went back to her weaving.

Ray went to the closet and took out a long, narrow box. "I got this for Lucy," he said softly. "I think she only used it once." He set it up in the bay window while Claire stood by, watching. She did not know how she should react. "Look," Ray said, flipping through the booklet that came with the telescope. "Try to find Cygnus. The manual says: 'Cygnus, a complex constellation, looks like a graceful swan spreading her wings against the night sky.'"

"I never knew astronomers had any imagination," Claire said as she leaned over to look into the ocular. She adjusted it for a few seconds, but she could not see anything. In that socket where a cluster of stars should have been, Claire could make out blackness only.

"Have you found Cygnus?" Ray asked, but she hadn't really been looking for it. She had begun to feel sad, for no apparent reason. It struck her how pathetic the whole situation was, this little makeshift group of people sitting in a faded living room. They were drawn together by a death, by shared, unspoken grief. Claire searched the night sky for any discernible movement. She thought of an oral report she had delivered in the fifth grade—or was it the sixth? It had been about comets, and she had drawn up an elaborate chart on oak tag for the occasion. Comets, she remembered, have been known to crack up into filaments when plunging earthward, with various particles landing in Ohio, in Wisconsin and on the soft floor of Lake Erie. She thought of this as she looked through the eyepiece, and the images moved her—it seemed that in the middle of all that heat and fuss there always had to be a kind of dispersion, an eventual separating of the elements.

Ray put away the telescope soon after, and Helen went around the rooms, shutting off lights. She did this every night before bed, darkening the house bit by bit. Claire stood in the living room, looking out the window. Ray had tried to be close to her in his own fumbling way. She was touched by it, but she did not know how to respond. That sort of kindness was not something she was used to. Whenever her parents acted nice to her, when they gave her a compliment or an extravagant present, one of them would always ruin the moment. "Go on, *open* it," her father had urged on Claire's nineteenth birthday as she cradled the wrapped package in her arms. So she ripped through the Day-Glo paper, accidentally tearing the gold rosette that had been affixed to the center. "Could you be a little more careful?" her mother said. "That bow might have been used again, you know. You never stop to think about anyone but yourself."

"I'm sorry," Claire mumbled, looking to her father for an ally. But he merely looked back silently, his eyes un-giving. The present was a beautiful solid-gold pendant, and when she wore it, it swung from her neck like a weight.

Her parents had lost all of their grace when Seth died. They were abrupt now, harsh. Claire did not really blame them; at least she understood where their fury came from, and she held back. They never tried to be close to her, but she excused them for that, too, thinking that such coldness could not last forever. One day, many years in the future, her parents would get lonely for their children and would reach out. Claire had no idea how she would react. It amazed her that she could be such an optimist in the midst of everything. No one would believe that a death girl could consider herself an optimist, not even the other death girls.

"Come off it," Laura would say, smirking. "What about Lucy Ascher's death landscape and all that? You've always told us that that's your world view, too, and now you want us to believe you're an optimist?"

"Yes," she would tell them, "I do live in a death landscape. But I never said I liked it, only that I had to live in it." Human nature was an entirely different issue. Claire had to have put some faith in it or she would not have gone to the Aschers'. If she did not trust human nature, then there wouldn't be much to go by. You could find only a limited number of things from old sepia photographs and diaries. You had to go beyond them, into the heart of things—into the sadness of Ray Ascher as he stooped to screw together the parts of the telescope. The need to be a parent was still in him. "See," he had said in a father's voice, "you fiddle with this to put things in focus. Try it."

It had made her want to cry. She saw how alone he was, how alone all three of them were. In the first several days she was there, she had not seen this; she had only experienced a kind of disorientation, a perpetual wondering about what she was doing in these strangers' home. The disorientation had eased a little when she fell into the routine of housecleaning. Each morning she made herself a light breakfast and unloaded the dishwasher. Ray would pad in when she was almost through, and she would heat up water for his coffee. Then she began work around the house, starting with the bedrooms upstairs and making her way down to the basement. She was left alone for most of the day. Ray went off to the college in midmorning, and Helen sat quietly in her favorite chair by the living room window or out on the freezing porch. All was silent in the house.

Now Claire's job had become ritual, and she moved through the rooms as though she had lived in them all her life. She knew where everything was kept, on which shelf Helen stored her compact sewing kit and the pincushion that looked like a strawberry, in which drawer of the hutch cabinet Ray had his magnifying glass and his shell collection. There was something touching about knowing the small particulars of other people's lives. When she was changing the sheets in Ray and Helen's bedroom, she noticed that Helen had left her wedding band on the night table. It was a thin gold ring, and Ray's and Helen's first initials were engraved on the inside. Helen wore the ring only every few days—Claire heard her tell Ray that she was afraid she might lose it. "After all, that almost happened once, remember?" Helen had said. She reminded him of the time her ring had slipped off her finger during some laboratory work at the college while she had her hand in the water of a draining tank.

Claire had not heard the beginning of this conversation, and she wondered what had prompted it. She could imagine Ray asking his wife why she hardly wore her wedding ring anymore. His ring was always on his finger. Perhaps, Claire thought, he could not get it off. She had read about cases like that—jewelry that had to be cut free from swollen-jointed fingers. Now *that* was real love, when your wedding ring was so much a part of you that it had to be cut free. Claire liked to think of small things like that as metaphors for larger concerns. She had always gravitated toward things that lent themselves well to metaphor. The idea of simile especially pleased her; the fact that something could be compared to something else in a way that was far-fetched and yet *true* made her feel that there just had to be a certain connectedness among all the things in the world. If you didn't believe that at all, then you were lost, left alone in the night to fend for yourself. This was one of the reasons that the death girls had so quickly banded together freshman year—each of them feared she could not go it alone. Without company, misery turns to sorrow, and sorrow turns inward, curling up in some dark, damp corner.

The death girls had a sort of buddy system going, like the kind used during free swim at Claire's old summer camp. The head counselor would blow shrilly into the whistle she wore on a lanyard around her neck, and the pairs of buddies would join hands and count off as they stood shivering in the waist-deep water. The death girls counted off each night, making sure that everything was okay and that no one was missing, spiritually speaking.

Claire felt good knowing that she was being taken care of, that she could share some of her thoughts and feelings with Naomi and Laura, but she also knew that this togetherness could go only so far. In the end, she realized, you were always by yourself. She remembered the first time this idea had occurred to her. She had been very small, and her parents had taken her and Seth to see the Ice Capades. They had managed to get front row seats and could see everything from up close. All of the skaters wore sequined costumes that shimmered two-tone under the lights, and colossal purple headdresses that looked like peacock tails at the Bronx Zoo. The skaters were just wonderful; they did cartwheels and back flips and leapt through ignited hoops. But the most exciting part of the evening was when they brought funny little cars out onto the ice and went around selecting children to ride in them.

All of a sudden one of the peacock ladies was standing in front of the Danzigers, holding out her electric arms, and Claire's mother and father lifted Claire up and out onto the ice. It was not slippery, as she had been afraid it might be. Instead it felt coarse under her feet, like walking on the grainy sawdust that was always sprinkled on the floor of the butcher's shop in Babylon. The lady helped Claire into the car, and they were off. They circled the rink in a blur three times, and at one point the lady lifted up Claire's hand and made her wave at the audience. She wondered how she would ever find her family again—as the car sped past she frantically scanned the tiers of faces for her parents and brother. She could not locate them, and for the first time in her life Claire understood that she was vulnerable to all the elements of the world. As the funny car was whisked along the ice, she felt as though she were rushing to her fate.

The ride ended soon after, and Claire was easily deposited back in her seat. She could only sit there, stunned, for the rest of the show. When the house lights went up, she pretended to have fallen asleep, and her father had to gather her up in his arms and carry her out to the parking lot.

———

S he knew she was making them happier. If not actually happier, then at least more hopeful. Helen's pace seemed quicker; she walked around the house as though she had a definite purpose, a direction. She was getting bored with her weaving, and unused beach grass was scattered around the rooms. Claire heard Ray tell Helen, "It must be this young blood in the house that's picking you up."

"Possibly," she answered.

You could hear so much in someone else's house. Even if you had not intended to eavesdrop, the voices rose up and filtered through the walls and under doors. There was a certain new vigor at the Aschers'. One morning Helen actually sat down and wrote out a short list of the things she wanted Claire to do. The list read:

> Defrost fridge.
> Re-paper kitchen shelves.
> Clean out Lucy's room.

Claire was shaken when she read the last item. She had not spent any time in Lucy's room before. She had been told it did not need cleaning, so there had been no real reason to go in. But once when Helen was in the bathroom, Claire went and stood in the doorway of Lucy's bedroom, her heart pounding. She opened the door slowly, expecting to see some kind of ascetic, inspiring sight: a writing desk with an exposed bulb for a lamp, dark peeling walls and a latticework of cobwebs in all the upper corners. But the room was an undistinguished girl's room: powder-blue carpet, white uncracked walls and ceiling, and a Rousseau print hanging over the bed. She heard Helen flush the toilet down the hall, and she quickly stepped out, closing the door behind her.

Now she had a legitimate reason to be there. Item three: Clean out Lucy's room. She could not imagine what the job included. She would save it for last, for the very end of the day. Only when she had defrosted the refrigerator and lined the kitchen shelves with clean new paper would she go upstairs to Lucy's bedroom. It was no secret place; it was not one of those rooms that could be reached only through a hidden sliding panel at the back of a fireplace. It was her own obsession that made it seem that way. What did she expect to find there, after all—another notebook, a sequel to *Sleepwalking*?

When Claire went up to Lucy's room at the end of the day, she sat down for a few minutes in the center of the carpet, getting her bearings. The room had obviously been gone through many times. It was also obvious that this was the room of someone who had died. Claire was an expert on this, having spent the last five years living in a house with such a room.

The bedroom of a dead child always had an artificial ambience. A selection of the child's belongings was arranged in a kind of order that strained to appear casual and random. Representative objects were lined up on the shelf in loving tribute. It was as though the parents were trying desperately to piece together a life, using whatever was available.

There had been a family of sparrows living on the ledge outside Claire's window at school freshman year, and she remembered feeling the same kind of hopelessness each morning as she watched the mother bird fly back and forth building up the nest, scraps of twine and pencil shavings dangling from her beak.

Claire stood up and began to look for things to do. She ran a rag over the furniture, and dust came off in a thick layer on the cloth. She moved the four-poster away from the wall and began to vacuum. She did not hear Helen come in because of the noise, but when she turned around she was there, leaning against the door. Claire shut off the vacuum switch with her foot. Its groaning died away, and the room was quiet. The two women faced each other.

"Claire," Helen said, "do you like it here?"

"Where?"

"In this room."

"Yes," Claire said, guarded.

"I thought you might want to move in here. It's bigger. You'd be more comfortable, I think." Helen's voice was subdued, and she was looking directly at Claire. She made her feel very tense.

A pulse jumped in Claire's neck. She paused, then said, "Okay. I'll get my stuff."

Helen smiled. "Good," she said, and she slipped out the door.

She was an odd woman, Claire thought. At first she had seemed aimless, but in the past two days she had been saying and doing things as though she had a purpose. Claire went down the hall to the guest room and got her things together. She didn't have much with her. She carried her clothes into

Lucy's room and stood with them piled in her arms, not sure of where she should put them. She slid open the top dresser drawer and placed some of her shirts next to Lucy's shirts. Side by side, the dark among the dark. She put everything away, and her own clothes took up exactly half of the dresser. She had some trouble closing the last drawer; it stuck on its runners for a second. She jammed it shut with the flat of her hand, and the whole room seemed to shudder at the vibration. The trinkets on the dresser top trembled.

"Lucy?" she said.

There was no answer. She was alone in the room; there was no other presence in there with her. The ghost seemed to have lifted from the house. She had felt it happening over the past few days, had felt it fading. She envisioned a showdown at dawn.

But that wouldn't happen. Claire had replaced the ghost of Lucy Ascher, and there was no real reason for it to hover overhead any longer. She hadn't even been aware of a competition until that moment. Now, alone in Lucy's room, she felt that she could stay there for a long time. She felt superior. She was living, she breathed more than cold, underground death air. The pulse in her neck jumped once again. She placed her fingers over it lightly, as though it were a cricket she was cupping in the grass.

Part 3

chapter twelve

Naomi the death girl came to his door late at night. Julian had been in the midst of a fretful sleep. He dreamed that he was running frantically down Fifth Avenue and that he was very late for the SAT exam. By the time he reached the building where it was being given, the students had just put down their No. 2 pencils, and the test was over. The proctor gave Julian an evil, satisfied smile. The knocking woke Julian at once and he leapt from his bed, glad to be free of the dream. He was wearing drawstring pajama bottoms and no top, and he felt very self-conscious as he let Naomi in. The room was completely dark and smelled of sleep. He turned on his desk lamp and then opened a window to air the place out. It was only after he had done these things that he began to wonder what she could possibly want with him.

"Oh, I woke you up," she said. "I'm really sorry."

"It's okay," he said, his voice still groggy.

She sat down on his desk chair while he sat on the edge of the bed. The lamplight made her look old. She bent her head and picked at a hangnail for a few seconds before speaking. He could see the dark roots in her bleached hair.

"I bet you're really surprised to see me here," she said finally. "We've been bitches to you, Laura and I. I promise you that's all over, as far as I'm concerned. I needed to talk to you tonight. You're the only one who would understand this. If you don't want to listen, though, just tell me and I'll go."

"I'll listen," he said. "It has to be about Claire. You know I'll listen to that."

"That's what I figured," Naomi said. "She called me tonight. At first I didn't even recognize her voice. She sounded kind of different, and I wasn't sure it was her. She called because she wanted to tell me that she's not coming back, and she said it defiantly, as if she wanted me to object, to make her leave."

"What do you mean?" Julian asked. "Why don't you just tell me where she is, to begin with, and then I can try to understand this stuff." He began to feel fully awake.

"Okay," Naomi said. "I wasn't going to tell you. I swore to Claire that I wouldn't say anything to anyone. But I have to break that promise because I'm all alone in this and I don't know what to do. Laura's off chanting in a closet or something."

"Tell me," Julian interrupted, his voice tight.

So she told him. She started from the beginning, from the night that the three death girls had sat on the floor and talked about getting their fill of their poets.

"We encouraged Claire," Naomi admitted. "We made her see that there were other things she could do if she really wanted to put herself into Lucy Ascher's life. I thought it would sort of, you know, exorcise the Lucy thing. Instead, all it did was throw her further into it. I never dreamed this would happen."

"What are you talking about?" Julian asked. "You come in here and wake me up and expect me to know what you're talking about. Where is Claire?"

"You'd better swear you won't ever tell her that I told you. Please, Julian. She'd never trust me again."

"Okay," he said. "I swear."

"She's there," Naomi said, "at the Aschers' house. She's been living with them as their cleaning woman."

Julian slid farther back on the bed, leaning against the wall. He ached to be at home, in his own room, with the headphones on, piping in the Grateful Dead. He would eat a wonderful dinner with his parents—baked chicken, asparagus shoots, sweet potatoes—and then wander upstairs into his own private domain. He would climb into his bed and listen to his favorite music until he fell asleep. In the middle of the night, he would feel someone—his mother, most likely—come in and slip off his headphones and disentangle the cord, careful not to disturb him.

He sat in his austere college room instead, facing a death girl. She was all in black, a midnight visitor, like death itself. "That is the weirdest thing I've ever heard," he said in a quiet voice. "I don't know how I get myself into these things."

"That's not the whole story," Naomi said. "That's not even

the weird part. I know it doesn't sound like the healthiest situation to you, but I still thought that Claire would be okay. I still thought that she'd be thinking clearly. When she called me tonight, I didn't know what to do. She started telling me about what's been going on, but it sounded as if it wasn't even her own life she was talking about. She told me that they really like her, that she fits in. First she was staying in the guest room, but a couple of days ago Mrs. Ascher had her clean out Lucy's old room, and then she told Claire that she could move her things in there if she wanted, that the bed was probably more comfortable than the one in the guest room. So now Claire is sleeping in Lucy's old room. It's as if she thinks she's turning into Lucy or something. I don't know what to do. She kept saying, 'Naomi, are you there?' over the telephone, because I couldn't speak—I didn't know what I was supposed to say to her. The whole thing sounded so *off* to me." She paused. "Do you think I'm overreacting?" she asked him.

Julian shook his head. "No," he said. He was so stunned that he had to wait a few seconds before he said anything else. Naomi seemed to understand. She didn't rush him but just let him take his time. Claire had gone too far; that was what all of this was about. While everyone else worried about her and practically ruined their lives over her, she was just doing as she pleased, he reflected. Claire was completely in charge of her life, as always. Julian suddenly felt hopeless about the whole thing.

"I think we'd better forget it," he said softly. "I don't know what else we can do."

Naomi lowered her head to her hands. "God," she said. "I feel completely alone in all of this."

Julian saw that she was about to cry. He didn't think he could bear that. "Well, look," he said quickly, "what about your friend Laura? You still have her, don't you? Why don't you talk about it with her?"

"No," said Naomi, shaking her head. "She's been really out of it these days. I don't know what's wrong with her. She's been seeing the shrink over at Health Services, and he gave her some Valium because she can't sleep at night. She's barely doing anything. She just lies around all day, depressed. I've tried to talk to her about Claire, but she's not interested. I'm really alone. I've been abandoned by my two best friends, and I don't even know why."

"I've been abandoned, too," Julian said. "I know that doesn't make you feel any better, but it isn't just you. Some people get wrapped up in themselves, and they forget about everyone else."

Naomi stood up. She looked taller than ever, with her head tilted slightly downward on her long, Mannerist neck. "I should let you go to sleep," she said. "This is really imposing on you."

"No," Julian said, "it's not." He suddenly didn't want her to leave; he wanted to reach out and touch her white blond hair. "Stay," he said. "Keep me company." He tried to smile, his old crooked smile. "I'm lonely too," he said.

They spent the whole night together, talking. He held her briefly in the beginning, and she put her hand on his head, then they both pulled away. It was too painful.

"Everything is so solemn in my life," Naomi said. "No matter what I do, it always ends up serious and really gloomy. I'm starting to hate that about myself. I just want to be able to actually enjoy something." She shook her head sadly. "I don't know that I ever will."

"I think you will," said Julian. "Things have already begun to change. The death girls have split up. How do you feel about it?"

"Very strange," she said, then smiled. "I can't believe it. I thought the three of us were going to grow old together— Claire, Laura and I. I thought we'd end up as a group of old crones living in the Barbizon Hotel for Women and carrying our life belongings in shopping bags." She paused. "Did you know that Sylvia stayed at the Barbizon when she was a guest editor at *Mademoiselle?*"

"No," Julian said. "I don't know much about Sylvia Plath."

She told him Sylvia had gone to New York and worked for the magazine. She told him that that was the summer the Rosenbergs were electrocuted. "It's in the first line of the book."

"What book?" he asked.

"*The* book," she said impatiently, "*The Bell Jar.*"

He confessed that he had never read it. She talked about the book, about how reading it had changed her view of the world forever. "Even now," she said, "when I find myself moving farther away from the whole death-girl thing, *The Bell Jar* still makes me look at life differently. When I was in high school, I read the book and it really shook me up. I was valedictorian of my class and a National Merit Scholar, and I suddenly realized that all the awards and prizes I'd been racking up meant absolutely nothing. Zilch. I'd been pushing ahead of everybody for years, like Plath, and I saw that none of it would mean anything in the long run, that I would die like everyone else."

He had not even asked her, and here she was talking about it, talking about her death-girl beginnings. Julian remembered the night in the library when Claire did the same thing. It was he who brought up the subject that time, but she had willingly taken over. The death girls seemed to need to talk about it. It was something intensely private, and yet it had to be released.

"Go on," he said to Naomi. "What happened then?"

"I was very alone for the whole summer," she said. "I just sat in the cabin my family had rented and read books. I couldn't wait until college began. I was very tempted to go to Smith—that's where Sylvia went—but part of me was scared. I thought if I went there, I might be following in her footsteps or something." She paused and said shyly, "I've always wanted to be a writer. Ever since I was very young. I've been keeping a journal for years. I look back over the pages of it, and I can even see how my handwriting has changed. If I went to Smith, I thought I might go off the deep end. Sylvia had a nervous breakdown after her junior year. She tried to kill herself when she came back from working at the magazine that summer. I can't believe you don't know this already—I thought everybody our age did. Maybe it's a universal female thing."

"I'm not sure about that," Julian said. He knew many women who didn't reserve special places in their hearts for a favorite doomed poet. He didn't think it had to do solely with being female; he thought it had to do with being alone. Maybe women felt alone more often than men, or maybe women just let it show more often. Julian had always liked to be by himself, but he had never felt isolated. There was something wonderful about sitting by yourself and just being able to think—not having to explain yourself to anyone. He used to ride the bus all the way up to the Cloisters when he was in high school. He would cut classes and bring along a sandwich and a piece of fruit and eat his lunch sitting on the stone wall that overlooked the quiet courtyard. He would sit there for much of the afternoon, feeling perfectly content. Now he thought about this, and for the first time he wondered if people who saw him there assumed that he was lonely. Did they shake their heads after they walked by and whisper to each other, "Poor kid"? There *was* something inherently lonely about a person alone in a public place, although he had never thought to apply this to himself before.

"What happened when you came to college?" Julian asked Naomi. "Did you feel less alone then?"

"Yes," she said. "I met Claire and Laura right away, and we hit it off. Soon we became a threesome—the chemistry was incredible. It was just what each of us needed to get through the year. Those early days . . . I still think about them sometimes and feel nostalgic and weepy."

"So where do you go from here?" Julian asked.

There was a pause. "I don't really know," Naomi said. "I'm at a loss." She shrugged. "How about you? What do you think about Claire? I assume you love her, or else you wouldn't be going through all this, but besides that, what do you really *think* of her? Why have we let her become so incredibly important to us? Sometimes I think there's something wrong with me, that I let myself get so attached to certain people."

"Yeah," Julian said. "I know what you mean. I've had that problem before, but it's worse now. Claire and I are so different. We have such different outlooks and everything. She thinks about death all the time, I just can't relate to it."

Naomi looked at him. "I wonder," she said, "if you'd be so crazy about Claire if she *wasn't* a death girl. I have a feeling that that's one of the things that draws you to her. I may be wrong—I can't read your mind."

He thought about it for a little while. Once again, Naomi did not rush him. It was already so late that they were beyond the point of caring.

"I don't know if it's that she's a death girl," Julian said. "Death girls have to be kind of secretive—at least the three of you come across that way—and I think it's the secretive part that interested me about Claire. Any time I see something I don't understand, I want to sit and work on it. It's like that man Levin Lucy Ascher wrote about in *Sleepwalking*—the mathematician she met at the mental hospital when she was twelve. When he had his nervous breakdown, he stayed up all night, working on math problems. He couldn't leave his desk, he just had to stay there and solve them. That scene really affected me. I never got to tell Claire that, because she hung up on me before I had the chance. I sort of related to it; I mean, I have the same kind of concentration that lets me just sit still for a really long time."

Suddenly he started talking about Claire in earnest. He told Naomi how intrigued he had always been by Claire. She was restless all the time. She always had to get up and move around in the middle of a conversation. She had to have a cigarette between her fingers, letting it burn down to a tiny stub. He once asked her why she liked to smoke, and she replied that she didn't like the act of smoking so much as she liked having something constantly burning in her hand, something to watch out for. "It keeps me attentive," she said.

Julian tried to calm her, to make her sit still. It was his project. Once he suggested that they meditate together. He didn't know much about meditation, but he figured he could fake his way through it. They sat down on the floor of her room, and he made her close her eyes. "Pretend that your body is a giant wind tunnel," he said. "When you breathe in, feel the air going softly down. When you breathe out, feel the air sliding from your body in a cool blue stream. Now inhale . . . slo-o-o-wly."

It had not worked. She had cracked open one eye within a few minutes and said, "God, I need to stretch." He had not given up, though. He tried to calm her, to soften her, by just being there. One night while he was reading in bed, she drowsed off next to him, her head on his hip. Soon she jerked from her sleep and moved over to her side of the bed. "I'm sorry," she said, turning away from him. He reached out to stroke her hair, to tell her he liked having her head there on his hip, that she could have kept it there all night—he wasn't uncomfortable in the least. She could not seem to understand that it was okay just to lie close and be still. She was tense all the time. He could feel it when he held her, the way her back was rigid when he looped his arms all the way around her.

"Claire's a true eccentric," he said to Naomi.

"What do you mean by that?" she asked.

He looked for words. "She's like a living paradox or something. I mean, she's so stiff, and still she manages to be overpowering. She always knows exactly what she's doing; she seems so self-contained, but at the same time it's like she's spilling out all over the place. I can't explain it any better than that."

But he didn't need to. Naomi nodded in a way that made him think she understood what he was saying. They were sitting very close to each other now, cross-legged, on the bed. She no longer seemed to him like death itself. She seemed overtired. The sky was getting light, and his next-door neighbor, who worked longer and harder than anyone Julian knew, had stopped typing and gone to sleep. Julian didn't look at the clock, but he knew it was very late. All of this over Claire Danziger. All of this worrying and missing sleep, and Claire wasn't even aware of it.

"Julian," said Naomi, "I don't think I can just forget it, like you said when I asked what we should do. It would make life simpler, I guess, but I just don't think I can do it. God knows what will happen. If she's really slipping into this Lucy Ascher life, she might never come out of it. I can't leave Claire like that."

"Neither can I," he admitted.

It was the Amish people who believed that when someone took your photograph, part of your soul was stolen away. He remembered the time his class at Dalton had taken a trip down to Pennsylvania Dutch Country and three young women in long skirts and huge bonnets had skittered off in a flock when someone in his class started to unscrew the lens cap from his camera. Julian understood how the Amish felt; he felt similarly about making love. After you slept with someone, she took away with her a small hunk of you. It wasn't bad, as long as the relationship went on. It was something you didn't mind giving up, because it would always be close by. It was only when things ended that you really felt the loss.

Julian had run into his old girlfriend Cathy in the city when he was home for Columbus Day weekend. She was a junior at Princeton and was walking down Central Park West arm in arm with a very tall blond man. "Julian, this is Kirk," she said.

Julian had muttered something about being glad to meet him and about how he hoped the rest of their year went well, and then he had pretended to be in a rush and hurried off down the street. It had embarrassed him to see Cathy. The first thing that had come to mind was their early, fumbling attempts at lovemaking. They had seen each other naked, exposed. They had told each other so many things—God, it embarrassed him even to think about it. Cathy had taken away with her a good many of his secrets, his most vulnerable moments. She had taken away a hunk of his soul.

He could picture her lying in Kirk's bed at college, telling him everything about the relationship that she had had with Julian. "He was so young and so well-meaning," she would say in that delicate voice of hers. "I was wide-eyed, too, I'll admit, but Julian was much worse. He always insisted on helping me put in my diaphragm, as if he thought I couldn't manage myself."

Julian could hear Kirk's deep, throaty, Princeton laugh. "Oh, that's priceless," Kirk would say.

Cathy had taken something of Julian away with her, and now, so had Claire. He knew that this would probably happen with all of the women he was ever involved with in his lifetime, but for some reason he felt that this time would probably be the most painful. He wanted it back—he wanted Claire back.

"We have to do something," he said to Naomi, and she quickly agreed. "It's really stupid to go on like this," he told her. "There has to be something else we can do."

"Yes," she said, "I know. We'll really have to work on it. Hard."

They sat in silence for a long time. He was remembering the way Claire had felt close up against him, a confusion of balances, with her arms lightly touching his shoulders and her tongue resting heavy in his mouth.

"Listen, you should go get some sleep," he said to Naomi.

"I guess you're right," she said. "I *am* starting to fall on my face."

They sat quietly for a few more minutes, and it struck him that this had been like one of the death girls' marathon sessions. Now he had some idea of what it really felt like, of where the joy and pain was in spending a whole night thinking and talking about someone you love, someone who is absent. It had been a full night. It had exhausted him.

Naomi stood up and got into her coat. Julian opened the door and ushered her out into the morning.

chapter thirteen

She could tell the thaw was somewhere in the distance. There were signs of it every year at this time. It was still cold but the water had somehow changed, smoothed itself out. "You know, I actually feel better," Helen said to Ray. It was odd to speak it, to acknowledge it. She had long ago given up the possibility of real change, and when it did come, it took her by surprise.

"I'm glad," he answered. "We should celebrate or something."

They were picking their way along the beach among snail skeletons, pebbles and worn-down shells. The water looked lighter than it had.

She turned and saw that Claire had lagged way behind them. Claire had opened and shut several times during the week. It was as though she wasn't sure how to act. She would relax for a moment, would comment on something, and then when Helen or Ray encouraged her to go on, she would catch herself and stop everything. It was as though she had to remind herself to keep a distance from them.

"Just leave her," Ray said, guessing Helen's thoughts.

"You can still read my mind," she said. They smiled at each other, and he reached for her hand. They walked along like that for another ten minutes. Helen didn't turn around, but even so, she could sense how listless Claire was. Every so often she could hear the plopping of small rocks that Claire was tossing into the water.

"Are you sure we should just leave her?" Helen asked. Ray nodded, and so they kept walking.

She was perplexed by Claire. Every day Claire stayed up in her bedroom—in Lucy's old room—late into the morning. There wasn't much work for her to do and Helen didn't care, but it made her uneasy. When Claire finally wandered downstairs to rummage through the refrigerator for yogurt or juice, Helen was usually sitting out on the cold sun deck. She would hear Claire coming down the stairs and would turn to watch her through the glass as she moved around the kitchen.

What a force Claire was in her silence. And what a familiar feeling, to look at Ray over Claire's head and shrug and have Ray shrug back. It sent something through Helen, the chill of déjà vu that can be instantly placed in time, in space. This was not one of those senses you have when you go somewhere new and think, I have been here before. I have stood on this hill, but I don't know when.

The déjà vu that Helen felt was instantly resolved. It did not shock her. She recognized that when Claire came to the house that day, something about her made Helen move to open the door and invite her in. Certainly she did not let in everyone who showed up outside. There had been those two giggling women once who wanted to know if Helen would talk to them about what Lucy was like as a baby, and there had been the serious, tailored woman who asked if Helen and Ray would like to be the keynote speakers at an annual dinner meeting of the Long Island Association of Bereaved Parents.

She didn't let any of these people in. She had been startled and shook her head at them and then backed up, softly closing the door. After she did this, her heart pounded. She felt an anxiety attack coming on each time and leaned against the shut door until she heard the sound of footsteps giving up and going away, retreating along the flagstone walk that Ray had laid when they first moved in.

With Claire, something had touched Helen—the need, probably, the plain show of desperation. Helen had spent so many years responding to these things in Lucy, grappling with them, not understanding them. It had almost become her role in life to do this, and she could not turn Claire away. Claire was a child, a young scared girl with an oversized suit-case. She was the baby in the basket left on the doorstep with a note tagged to one wrist: "Take care of her for us, please. We know you can do it better than anyone else."

At the very least, it was ironic. Helen and Ray had certainly proved themselves to be incompetent as parents, although their friend Len Deering had assured Helen that it was not as simple as all that. "You can't just say, 'I have failed as a mother,'" he told her. "There are so many other factors involved. Lucy was a grown woman. It's very hard, and you have a lot of exploring to do, but after a while you're just going to have to let go."

Letting go. It was such an easy phrase. It brought to mind a series of wonderful images: a dam bursting forth into a spill of clean, flowing water, a kite string being unraveled into the sky, or a couple arching their backs in the middle of making love, one of them looking up and calling out in rapture, "Now!"

It was too easy. Letting go also meant other things, things people never discussed. There were restrictions; everything always had to be cathartic these days. In the supermarket one day the summer before, Helen had heard a woman saying to a friend as the two of them peered over the frozen-foods counter, "I'm taking a jazz dance class. It's real therapy for me."

What about the other side of letting go, the side that stuck closest to the words themselves? When you really let go, you were saying goodbye forever. No one ever wanted to talk about that aspect; it was universally considered too painful. It didn't seem as if anyone came to terms with the real business of letting go. You just gradually loosened your grip, and after a while you simply forgot that you were holding on. That was what Helen had started to do with Lucy. Somehow, it had eventually happened. Helen had woken up and been too exhausted to think about her. She usually lost herself in such thoughts each morning.

She remembered as she lay in bed that Claire was fast asleep in Lucy's old room. She wondered if she was warm enough. There were two blankets on the bed, but they were fairly thin. The night before, when the temperature suddenly dropped, Claire had assured her that she would be fine, but still Helen worried. Claire's stance made it seem as though she were constantly trying to prove that she needed no protection, and it was this that drew Helen to her. Lucy had done the same thing, had tried so hard to appear deadpan, and Helen had wanted to rush to her, to change her, to hold her.

Having Claire in the house brought out these feelings all over again. It did not make Helen feel worse, though, as she had thought it might. It occupied her; it gave her a project to work on. She and Ray had shared almost nothing in years. Grief didn't count, because in a way it *was* nothing; there wasn't anything in it to hold on to, just wide-open, empty space.

When Lucy was alive, she couldn't be figured out, no matter how hard Helen or Ray tried. She was solidly there, but she was made up of all smooth edges. You couldn't hold her. So instead, Helen and Ray had held each other. In the old days, they made love after coming back from the lab, both of them stinking of shared chemicals. Helen knew that having each other did not compensate for their emptiness with Lucy, but it helped.

When Lucy died, Helen and Ray did not continue to move closer together. There was a point in life when you had to remain separate, when you could not share anything more. Helen bought an electric blanket at Sears for them that first winter after the death, and it had two individual heat controls. Ray would turn his side way up to High, and Helen would keep hers on Low, so even their bodies were in different terrains, polar opposites.

Everything was unspoken. She thought of Lucy as a child, and she thought of her muteness that summer, such a long time ago. It had confounded Helen then and remained a mystery throughout the years. But now, with Claire in the house, she thought she finally understood what it was to be unable to speak but to want to desperately. That was how Claire was— always on the brink of saying something, then pulling back. Lucy had been the same, and Helen had done nothing about it. She had not yanked her depressive daughter by the collar and made her talk, made her unload all the secrets she had been storing up for a lifetime.

In the two years since Lucy's death, Helen also had been unable to speak, unable to tell Ray how she felt. She had really not wanted to. What could he possibly have said? He would have nodded and stroked her shoulders and back with his huge, warm hands, and it would have actually felt *good*, and she would have hated herself for responding so dumbly to touch.

She heard Claire waking up. A couple of pronounced yawns, the rustle of covers, then the swing and thump of feet over the side of the bed. Helen felt the way she used to feel— she had an urge to get up and meet her daughter in the hallway, to watch the stagger of waking up, the sweetness of a child still drunk with sleep.

She made herself stay in bed. It would seem odd if she were to go out and stand in the hall, waiting. Claire would look at her with unblinking eyes, and Helen would be embarrassed.

She stayed under the blanket with Ray asleep in his warm patch next to her. "Ray?" she said, touching one finger to his chest.

It was the way she had always wakened him, ever since the beginning of their marriage. After a while he would feel the extra bit of pressure there and wake up. It took him several seconds this time, then he reached out in his sleep to brush her finger away. She did not move her finger, and soon he reached for it again, and this time he held it for a moment, trying to figure it out. It reminded her of the parable of the three blind men and the elephant. Ray moved from her finger to her hand and then up to her arm. He opened his eyes, and he was holding her elbow in a formal way, as though he were escorting her to a ball.

"Good morning," she said.

"Good morning."

He let go of her elbow and turned over onto his back. He stretched out his arms and legs—she could hear tiny bone explosions, as though he were cracking his knuckles. "Ray?" she said again.

"What?"

"I was wondering what you think of her."

"Claire?" he said, yawning. "She's all right."

That was the end of it for the time being. They lay there together without moving. She could hear Claire walking around and doing morning things. There were the sounds of the window shade being whisked up, and a few seconds later, the shower being turned on.

It was ludicrous, all of it. Helen wanted very much to tell

Claire what was happening, just how she was feeling with her in the house. She sat up and moved to the edge of the bed, stepping into the flattened green slippers that waited there on the floor each morning.

"You're going?" Ray asked, his hand on her spine.

"I'm restless," she said. "I want to get up." She turned to look at him. She was aware of the way her breasts swung around as she turned; she could feel the shifting of their weight. Her nightgown was almost diaphanous. It had not looked that way in the store. It just seemed light and easy to wash, so she bought it. For years clothes had been covering, nothing more.

Ray regarded her breasts through the material. This deeply embarrassed her, as though she and Ray were teenagers all over again, sitting half naked on a grassy rise and looking at each other but pretending to be looking out at the lights of the Brooklyn Bridge, which formed a loose star chain in the night.

She had to go to Claire.

She walked down the hallway, and the shower was still running. She sat down on the carpeted step and waited. Soon the water was shut off, and she could hear a few last drops spattering down.

There was a squeal of curtain rings being shoved along the rod as Claire stepped out. The door opened a few minutes later, and the bathroom was like a tropical rain forest, steaming and lush with exotic plant smells. Herbal Essence shampoo, probably. Claire stood in the doorway with a thick yellow towel wrapped around her middle. She looked as though she had just forged her way through the rain forest and made it safely out into the dry sun, the forest still wet and alive behind her.

Helen thought that Claire must have been mystically sent to them. She had had that feeling with Lucy, the same bewilderment. Perhaps it was a naïveté—Helen was reminded of all those cases of women in Appalachia who go to the doctor because their stomachs hurt and then find out that their stomachs hurt because they're really six months pregnant.

Helen did not wonder at the act of birth itself—that had always seemed too grueling and stark to be anything other than earthly. Everything in the delivery room had been hospital-green, and in the background a nurse was endlessly telling her to bear down harder. There was a painless snip of her skin, a tearing that eased the way, and after all the open-mouthed panting, she felt the baby's head crowning. Crowning—it was such a wonderfully apt word for a baby who was going to be at the center of everyone's life for years, sitting calmly each day in its highchair throne.

Helen could not understand how babies turned into whom they did; she did not see where any of it came from. Throughout the years, Helen and Ray had looked at seashells and tried to interest Lucy in them. She had remained impassive. When they held out a conch to her and invited her to come look, she would barely glance at it before turning and trotting back to whatever she was doing—drawing concentric circles with her finger in the sand or sitting in the shade of the porch reading a book. That was why it was startling when Lucy grew up and wrote poetry, and her poems were filled with references to shells, to the ocean. Had she been studying them on the sly all those years? In her first collection, there was a whole cycle of poems devoted to sea anemones. Helen was surprised at the accurate, good detail in every line.

She telephoned Lucy after she read the manuscript and asked, "When did you learn all that?"

"When you weren't looking," Lucy answered stiffly.

It was the kind of response that you had to toy around with all day in order to understand. What did it really mean? Was Lucy implying that Helen hadn't been a good mother, that she hadn't been watching when she was supposed to? It upset Helen, but she did not broach the subject again. She did not want to disturb Lucy, not when her book was coming out. She seemed so shaky all the time, and Helen did not want to add to it. Lucy was living in New York, in a tiny, dim apartment in the West Village. Every time Helen and Ray came to visit they would bring with them a couple of potted plants. The apartment hardly got any light, and Lucy usually forgot to water the plants, so they soon died. She didn't move the clay pots from their places on the sill, and crumbled brown leaves littered the floor underneath the window like spilled tobacco.

"Sweetie," Helen said the first time she came to visit after Lucy moved in, "why don't you fix the place up a little?"

"It's the way I like it," Lucy answered, leaning back against the cold silver radiator. She stayed like that for several minutes, with her bare feet crossed in front of her, her head tilted up. It was as though she were challenging them.

Ray touched Helen's arm. "Don't," he said to her in a soft voice, meaning: Don't anguish over this.

He had done that sort of thing right from the start, when

things first began to go bad. The day Lucy stopped talking, Helen had called him up and had him come home in the middle of a class. He had said it to Helen as he stood next to her in Lucy's bedroom. Lucy was crouched in a corner of the room, wedged between the bedstead and the wall. Helen stood there, stunned, shaking her head slowly back and forth.

"Don't," he said, his hand on her arm.

She had not known what to do when she found Lucy huddled there. She had started thinking about people going into shock, and how you weren't supposed to move or even touch them. Maybe that was what had happened to Lucy: shock. You were supposed to call somebody—the doctor, an ambulance. But Helen had not wanted to do that; there was something, a kind of terrified look in Lucy's eyes, that made Helen want to have Ray there with her. She had dialed the department. The secretary walked down the hall into Ray's classroom and told him he was wanted at home. He had been about to administer a quiz on algae, and when he canceled it and packed up his briefcase hurriedly, all of his students had cheered.

Helen was always struck by the innocence of young girls. It really didn't have much to do with experience, it was just a certain look that all of them had. When Helen went into the hospital one winter for a routine D&C, there had been a young girl in the next bed who was there for an abortion. When the nurses brought her back after it was over and made her sit up and get ready to leave, she had said in a tiny, sleepy voice, "Oh, couldn't I stay in bed a little longer?" She was no older than fifteen, and Helen thought she sounded like a small child begging to sleep a few moments more before getting up for school.

The girl's parents stood slope-shouldered in their overcoats in the doorway, silently waiting to take her home. Helen had turned to face the wall so she would not have to watch anymore.

It didn't mean much to be a parent. All of those books—advice from Dr. Spock and the rest of them—could take you only so far. They told you how to make the baby stand and take its first steps like a little sleepwalker, arms stretched out in front for leverage. They told you the right way to mix up the food, to mash together the greens and oranges and yellows into a muddy paste and spoon it in so it got swallowed. Here comes the train, choo-choo, speeding around the tracks, clickety-clack, and into Lucy's mouth. Open the tunnel wide and let the train through. *That's* a good girl. They told you a few basic tenets of child psychology. They told you what was the right allowance to give a child at each age; there was even a chart. They told you how to make your child feel independent. How to give your child responsibility. A pet, perhaps, a small one at first. Lucy had overdone it with nine hamsters. She had gotten them from her third-grade class at school. The mother hamster that lived in a cage by the window had given birth once again, and there were too many animals in the classroom. The metal exercise wheels squeaked all the time and distracted the children from their lessons, so the teacher asked if anybody would like to take a couple of the hamsters home as pets. Lucy had somehow ended up with nine. She brought them into the house in a shoe box, and a couple managed to nudge their way out and run all over the place. Helen had to chase them around the kitchen, dropping a colander to the linoleum as a net. One of the hamsters disappeared completely, and the whole family searched the house for an entire morning. Ray moved the sofa away from the wall and knelt with a flashlight in front of every open closet. Lucy searched the house with her parents, but she did it dispassionately, as though she were looking for something she did not want to find, like a poor report card that needed to be signed by a parent and brought back to school. The hunt ended when there were no obvious places left to look.

A few weeks later, when Helen was vacuuming in the living room, she found the lost hamster lodged in the bottom of the wall, where a small chunk of molding had come loose. It had crawled its way into the darkness and died in a nest of electrical wire. Helen took out the hard little body in some bunched-up newspaper and buried it in the sand. She never told Lucy about it, and Lucy never asked. She didn't seem to care what had happened to it. As far as Lucy was concerned, the hamster had simply vanished. It might have sprouted little furry wings and flown away.

You couldn't raise a child to love life. You just had to cross your fingers and hope that it would happen naturally. *Life is good*, you subtly had to drum into your child's ears, bolstering the message by displays of love and affection. You had to hold your child, and you had to be unafraid of holding your spouse in front of your child. Helen and Ray were embracing once when Lucy came into the room. Ray started to break away, but Helen held him there for a few more seconds. She wanted Lucy to see the love that stirred between her parents, to see that it was a good thing. Lucy had barely been interested. She looked up at them with a slightly annoyed expression. "Are you going to fix my lunch or not?" she asked.

When Lucy was eighteen, she had her first love affair. It was with a Columbia student who was in her English class. She told her parents about it calmly when she came home for a weekend. "I've been sleeping with someone," she said over dinner.

So perhaps something had gotten through to her. Perhaps she had seen that she could not be autonomous in life, that she needed other people. Helen hoped the relationship would last. She told Lucy that she could bring the boy home any time she wished. But things ended quickly, and Lucy said she had never really liked him, anyway. She retreated into herself even more and barely finished her first year at Barnard. A couple of weeks into the summer she slit her wrists.

Do you love death more than you love life? Helen had wanted to ask as she stood at the foot of Lucy's hospital bed. It was an inconceivable thought, and she could not even start to concentrate on it.

Helen always felt an odd drive when she saw young girls on the street. She wanted to stop them, to grasp them by the arms and give them a few words of sound, lifelong advice. But the thing was, as soon as the girls drew near enough so that Helen could see their faces, she realized that they looked as if they were doing all right without any outside help. Young girls came in packs these days, wearing skimpy sequined T-shirts and wedge heels. They had one another, they had their friends, their boyfriends. They had their own parents to give them advice, so Helen passed by quickly, not saying a word.

Claire wasn't like that at all. There was no giddiness to her, none of that typical adolescent spark. Helen sat and looked at Claire, who was fresh from the shower. She had wanted to say something but had forgotten what it was. Helen wondered what kind of childhood Claire had had before her brother had died and how old she had been when it happened.

Helen had known from the beginning why Claire had come to the house. Claire was not much different from the women who wrote letters, who telephoned, who sent over baskets of fruit and preserves and smoked cheeses. This was what it was like, being the parent of someone famous and young, someone who was a suicide. How good a poet had Lucy actually been? Helen had no way of knowing. Lucy had received a lot of attention because she was so young. Her work was included in several anthologies, one of them a collection of contemporary poems written by women, entitled *I Hear My Sister Calling*. She would have hated that title, Helen thought. Lucy had always hated anything that involved a group, anything that involved real sharing.

"Mom, I don't feel a kinship with anyone," Lucy said to her once. She said it with a certain degree of pride in her voice, and Helen had felt sad.

Lucy had been poet-in-residence at Columbia when she was twenty-two. The only people who still remembered that year keenly were the unhappy ones. They were the people who felt that Lucy was speaking exclusively for them, the malcontents of the world in their dark, narrow rooms. Lucy had fueled the dreams of adolescents and those who had never grown out of adolescence. The whole thing was messy, and Helen wished desperately that Len Deering was right, that there was a way of letting go. She was going to try to find one. You have to trick yourself, she thought, in order to make yourself believe it is possible.

She sat on the stairway and looked up at Claire. There was a good deal left unsaid and much meaning in that stern, hard face flushed from the steam of the shower. Yet this ungiving young woman, this stranger, actually made Helen feel better. She comforted her. Helen stood up and reached out her hand, touching Claire's hair. Claire stared, then pulled away. Of course. What was it Helen had wanted to say? She remembered then, as she stood there. "Claire," she said, "I'm glad you're here."

Claire did her best to smile. She said something low, under her breath, that Helen could not hear. Then she turned and went into her room, leaving a trail of wet footprints on the hall carpet.

"You'll start feeling better only when you're ready to," Len Deering had said, and now she thought that was probably valid. You could not begin to feel better unless you were prepared to take on the responsibilities that went along with becoming a social being. Helen and Ray would have to invite the Wassermans over to dinner one night. Somehow that didn't seem like all that bad an idea. Jan Wasserman would lug along a huge kettle of fresh bouillabaisse, and it would be hot and good. They would sit around the Aschers' dining-room table, eating and exclaiming over the food. They would put on some music and retreat to the living room and look out on the water, as though it were an entirely new landscape.

People always talked about the sea as unpredictable, always in flux. In graduate school one of Helen and Ray's friends had said, "The reason I like studying the ocean is because it's like doing something different every day." The idea had thrilled Helen. She loved to think of things that way.

She had never been as quick to grasp scientific concepts as Ray. Certain things stayed with her, though. When she first began learning about the ocean, she had loved studying plate tectonics—continental drift. It was wonderful to think that huge land masses might be moving apart and shifting deep under the surface of the earth, even as she and Ray slept. Profound things happened when you weren't looking, and there were times when you couldn't look, when you had to close your eyes for a moment of private darkness.

When Lucy died, Helen could hardly force herself to go near the water. Lucy had jumped from a bridge, and a trawler had scraped along the bottom to drag her up. Her eyes were wide open, her eyelashes flecked with sand. The men covered her body with a bright orange emergency blanket.

Helen stayed in the bedroom with the shades pulled down so she could not see the water those first days when the death was new. She still heard it, though, and she put show music on the stereo to block out the sound of the waves.

But now she felt different—restless. She had needed solitude before, the comfort of a dark room and washcloths dipped in iced tea and placed over her eyes. Now Claire was here, and Helen wanted to talk to her, to do something for her. The other evening the three of them had played a long game of Scrabble. It had been Ray's idea. He rummaged through the top of the hall closet and retrieved the shabby maroon box. "Want to play?" he asked. He had to urge Claire to leave her room and join them.

They sat in the kitchen and played until very late. Helen won, after using all her letters to make "CAVERNS" on a triple-word square, and Claire came in second. Ray had never been very good with words. He couldn't form them quickly; even when he was talking, he had difficulty. He could not express himself well—he mumbled and usually gave up. Helen knew that she had not been as good a listener as she could have been. She sometimes drifted off when Ray was talking, as though his words were the lyrics to some gentle lullaby. She could not help herself.

In the middle of the game, when it was Ray's turn and he had been taking a long time to arrange his tiles, Helen looked up and realized that there was an ease to the room, the kind that is usually generated only after people have been living together for years and years. Claire had been with them for just two weeks, and yet she sat in the kitchen, hunched over the board, with the look of someone who had grown up in the house.

Everything was subtle, and that was why it did not seem as though it had happened quickly. Claire was here with them, sitting in Lucy's old chair, and oddly enough, none of it was surprising. Ray had said it best, the first night Claire was in the house. "She fits," he said, and while Helen pretended not to react, to be thinking about something else, she had known that he was right.

She thought about people who had no children. She had

known one such couple. When anyone questioned them on this subject, they would reply that they did not need a child, they had each other. Helen had been impressed by this sureness. How could you know that your marriage would not sour years later? How could you be positive that you would not need someone else in the house to keep you happy, someone small and warm to keep you sane?

It was Claire's presence that made Helen feel rooted, grounded in her old life. After the Scrabble game ended that night, Claire went upstairs and Helen and Ray stayed in the kitchen for a while. Ray opened a bottle of sherry that had been standing untouched in the closet for months. He had come home with it one day, anticipating, Helen imagined, a time in the future when they would want to drink it. A time when they would lift their glasses by the stems and clink them gently together. Claire was humming upstairs, and Ray uncorked the dark bottle, and they drank.

"To whatever," he said, touching his glass to hers.

They sat at the kitchen table for another hour, drinking and talking. "Let's take a day trip soon," he said.

"Okay," said Helen. "I'd like that. I've been getting kind of stir-crazy."

"I can tell," he said. "It's a good sign."

The humming stopped. Helen leaned back in her chair and craned her neck to see into the upstairs hallway. The light in Claire's room was off, or else the door was closed—possibly both. The sherry had made Helen feel very tired and overheated. "Feel my face," she said, taking Ray's hand and placing it flat against her cheek.

"Hot," he said.

They were sitting very close together at the table, and she could smell his aftershave—something with pine in it—and the sherry on his breath. The white overhead light was harsh, nothing was hidden. It was a light to cut food finely by, to read recipe print by. Now she could see his pores and all of the deep creases in his face. They shared responsibility, that was certain. They had been married a long time, she thought, leaning against him.

"Whoa," he said, thinking she was a little bit tipsy and had lost her balance. He braced her shoulder, and then she turned her face up to his, expectant.

chapter fourteen

She saw them dancing from the top of the stairs. At first she did not know what they were doing. She saw a whirl of bodies and heard music blaring on the stereo, but she did not connect these things with dancing.

Claire walked down the stairs and stood in the entrance to the living room. It was then that she realized they were waltzing. Ray was holding his wife very close and twirling her around in circles. They were laughing as they moved. Every once in a while Helen would turn her head slightly to the side to make sure they weren't about to tip something over, like the huge china vase in the corner or the antique end table which stood on thin nineteenth-century legs.

Claire was standing a few yards away from them, and they had no idea she was there. The music ended, and Ray went to change the record. He took a thick vintage disk from the stack next to the stereo and said to Helen, "Wait till you hear this." It was a tango.

"Ray," she said, "come on. I can't do that."

But he would not listen to her. He grabbed her by the waist and pulled her close up to his body. Soon she was dancing with him in perfect tango form. Her left cheek was flush against his right as they moved in Claire's direction, still not seeing her. Helen had an odd expression on her face, as though she were clenching an imaginary rose between her teeth.

Claire felt embarrassed, watching them. It was a very private moment, and there she was, standing in the doorway. Suddenly she felt as if everything were way over her head, far beyond her reach. During Orientation Week at Swarthmore she had sat next to two physics enthusiasts at breakfast, and when the conversation grew technical and incomprehensible, Claire felt herself being swallowed up. There had been no place for her there, so she had picked up her tray and left the cafeteria without eating.

Watching Helen and Ray dancing, she wondered if it was time for her to leave them. It was not a feeling of insecurity; it was something else, which she could not fully understand. It was the kind of sadness that comes when you realize something has come to a quiet end, and are surprised that it has. She thought of all the corny movies she had seen and books she had read in which the husband walks out on the family—just packs up a few of his belongings, touches the foreheads of his wife and young children as they lie sleeping, and then walks out the front door and down the long dirt road. You cannot hold people together if they do not belong together. It may work for a while, but then things begin to fall apart—there is silence and restlessness, and you know it is time for someone to leave.

Is death like that? she wondered. Do you get summoned— a light brush on your shoulder or a dimming of your vision, and do you calmly and sadly accept it? Does life leak from you gradually, so that you have time to watch it go?

She hadn't been at the hospital the night Seth died. She had been at a movie by herself. Her father had given her some money and sent her off. "Take a break," he said. "We'll be with him." And so she had gone to see a comedy, and sometime in the middle of it Seth had died. Her father wasn't outside the theater to pick her up when the movie let out, as he was supposed to have been. She waited awhile, and all the cars left the parking lot. Then one of their neighbors pulled up to the curb. She saw him, and she suddenly knew. Her parents had sent him to pick her up; something had happened. "Claire," said Mr. Getz, leaning across the seat and calling to her from the window. He did not say another word, and she opened the door and climbed in.

It saddened her that she hadn't been there. Her parents told her it had been a quiet death; he had been sleeping, or had at least been in a sort of drug-sleep, and everything had finally given way. It was incomplete to her, though. There had to have been something more, some nuance her parents had missed. Maybe a shadow had passed over the room, or maybe there had been a breeze floating in through the window. She wished she had been there to see.

Now Claire stood and continued to look at Helen and Ray.

They had their arms draped around each other in a way that indicated that they had been dancing partners for years. There was an ease to the way they moved. When they saw Claire they smiled awkwardly. "Just getting some exercise," Ray called out to her. His voice was lost under the strains of the tango.

Claire went into the kitchen and began to work in time to the music. She sponged down the copper tiles which lined the wall above the sink. She knew that she could work as much or as little as she wished; it did not matter to Ray and Helen. They scarcely seemed to notice how often she cleaned anymore. They still watched her, but it was in a way that was different than it had been in the beginning.

The other evening, just after Claire had climbed under the covers to go to sleep, she heard a faint tapping at her door. "Come in," she called out in the darkness, and Ray and Helen entered the room.

"We wanted to see . . . if you needed an extra blanket or anything," Ray said.

"No," Claire answered. "I'm fine."

They did not leave for a few seconds. They loomed over the bed like angels, like parents. She could not make out their features; they appeared in silhouette, back-lighted against the brightness from the hallway. Claire felt very small as she lay there.

"Good night, sweetie," Helen said. This startled Claire, but before she could even take it in fully, the Aschers had slipped from the room.

She had come to them when they needed her. Her timing could not have been better. There was a certain point during the course of extended grief when one had to have a change, something had to be filled in. She knew this from watching her own parents. It was roughly a year and a half after Seth died that her mother and father joined a local bridge club. The group met every Wednesday night at a different couple's house. Claire remembered how her parents talked about nothing but bridge during the month they were in the club. Their conversation was fevered; they had worked themselves up to a state in which they believed they were being renewed. They felt that their lives were starting all over again, and the prospect was overwhelming.

"Well," her father would say during dinner, squinting in concentration, "if declarer had tried to prevent a spade ruff, it wouldn't have worked. He could return a trump, but it wouldn't have done any good."

"Why not?" her mother asked, scribbling furiously on the pad of paper next to her glass. "It looks to me as if it would be all right."

"Look, we'll go over it again." And then they would talk about it for the rest of the meal while Claire sat in silence.

Then one night her father got into an argument with one of the other players, a man who lived three blocks away. The group was meeting at the Danzigers' house that night, and from upstairs Claire could smell coffee brewing and hear her father say, "Diamonds! I *said* diamonds!"

She heard her mother murmur something to him, but it didn't seem to help. In a minute her father's voice was loud and strident, and the bridge game broke up soon after. Her mother came upstairs to fetch the coats, which had been thrown onto the bed. She passed by Claire's room with a pile of them slung over her arm and said, "Why aren't you asleep?"

Claire could hear the sound of car engines being started. After the last couple drove away down the street, her parents began to have it out. Her mother lashed at her father, and he yelled back. Their voices volleyed back and forth. It seemed to be a prelude to something stronger—an exchange of slaps, maybe. Her father had hit her mother once. Claire remembered it very vividly. She and Seth were young—she even recalled that they were both wearing Dr. Dentons that night; they used to play ice skaters on the floor of the kitchen, gliding across the linoleum on their smooth plastic pajama-feet soles.

It had been a fight about money. Her father was accusing her mother of spending too much of it. Claire was not frightened—the subject was always raised on *I Love Lucy*. Lucy would spend more than they could afford, and Ricky would lower his head and flare his nostrils like a raging bull and say, "Looocy . . . " Claire thought that this was just another facet of marriage. She thought all marriages were like this. It was only when she heard the slap that she was shaken. It was a clean sound, a punctuation. She and Seth looked at each other, afraid. There was a pause downstairs, an awful stillness, and then her mother said in a new, low voice, "Well, that's just great. You should be really proud of yourself now."

Things ended there. Her mother walked slowly upstairs, her palm pressed to the side of her face. She went silently past Claire and Seth. Downstairs her father went into the kitchen and got out a tray of ice cubes from the freezer. She could hear the dry cracking as he bent back the plastic spine. He carried the ice upstairs to his wife. As he passed by Claire and Seth, he too was silent. There was no more noise that night.

After the bridge game, the argument was short and ended without resolution. There was no slapping this time, no throwing of objects. Claire imagined that her parents must have faced each other in the living room and suddenly thought, *My God, what are we doing?* There was such rage inside them— only when it surfaced could anyone know the extent of it. They were furious because they realized that trumps and dummies and contracts could not change anything, could not take away their sadness. Release did not come from diversion.

Did it come from replacement, though? That was what Claire was at the Aschers' house. She was a substitute—if you squinted hard and did not listen too closely, she could almost pass for Lucy Ascher. She knew it. She sat huddled in the chair in the corner of the den. This was her morning break from cleaning the house—sitting in the easy chair where Lucy must have sat countless times. The sea played shadows on the wall that faced the windows. Claire sat underneath these shadows, letting them pour over her. Helen and Ray Ascher went out on a day trip that morning. "We'll be back by three," they said to her. "See you later."

"See you," she said, turning away.

The Aschers were springing slowly to life like those crumpled crepe-paper balls you drop into water and watch as they open into flowers. Paper flowers.

Claire was not sure she trusted this change in Helen and Ray, this new bloom. It was too quick, she thought. Helen and Ray had come together, had collided, it seemed, surprised at finding themselves so close. She sensed that they had not really talked to each other in a long time. She wondered if they ever made love anymore.

As they left the house for their drive they laughed softly, sharing some private joke. What was funny, Claire wanted to know. She looked around her and she saw darkness, all the trappings of a dark world, another death landscape.

Before, she had felt sorry for the Aschers because of their grief. Now she felt sorry for them because of their twinges of hope. Claire knew it was wrong to deny anyone hope. Hope was everything. Hope pulled the most hopeless cases up and out of their deathbeds. That was what people had said about Seth. "Have hope, have faith." This was uttered so often that it was like a litany, a jump-rope song. Claire could not go through that another time. It had taken too much out of her; it had sapped her completely. The antidote lay in becoming a part of what frightened you most, so that you would not be discernibly affected by it.

A few months after Seth's death Claire had found herself walking in a seedy part of New York City. She had not been paying attention to where she was going. She had walked without stopping for an hour, and it was then that she realized she was no longer in a good part of the city. The block was empty except for a few men walking toward her from across the street. There was something strange about them; they were making weird noises and calling out things to her. Claire was frightened. The day was growing dark, and there was no one around she could call to for help. As the group approached her, she simply pretended to be one of them, twitching and muttering and looking for trouble, and so they left her alone. She had never forgotten the lesson.

The Aschers were gone for most of the day. In the middle of the afternoon, when she had finished a load of laundry and was stretched out on the living-room rug, floating in and out of a light sleep, she heard footsteps coming up the front path and assumed the Aschers had returned. But there was a knocking on the glass instead of a key turning in the door. Claire sat up and shook herself awake. "Who is it?" she called, but there was no answer.

She had not been alone in the house for a significant length of time before. Helen usually went out of the house only when she had to. Today was the first time she had decided to go out for no real reason. Ray had been elated. At breakfast that morning he had asked her where she would like to go. "We could take the ferry to Shelter Island," he said. "Or we could go to Montauk. Whatever you like."

"It doesn't matter," she answered. "I just want to get out; that's all I care about. It'll feel good to be somewhere else."

The only other place Helen had gone to recently was the supermarket. She did her grocery shopping on Tuesday afternoons, and she had asked Claire to accompany her the previous week. They did not say a word to each other during the drive to the store. Helen switched on the radio, and a concerto came in faintly. They both sat and listened to classical static. At the supermarket Helen seemed at ease. She wheeled her cart gently up and down the aisles, and she plucked things off the shelves without thinking about it. Claire tagged along behind her like a child. Helen hadn't really needed her there, Claire knew. Helen was lonely, and she wanted company. She wanted Claire's company.

Claire had come to the Aschers' house so that she could have the time and place to reflect on things. On the train out to Southampton the first day, she had let herself branch off into some crazy thoughts. She imagined Lucy's dreams hanging in the air of the house like old laundry, waiting for someone to come along and dream them all over again. She imagined that she would be able to enter into Lucy's thoughts, into the heart of her fears.

It had not happened. But what *had* happened was nebulous. She had derived something from living there, but she was not at all sure what it was. She knew only that she felt at home. At first she had felt close to Lucy, to the ghost of her. But then, as the days passed, Claire had taken over, and Lucy was gone. Claire had never meant that to happen.

The knocking at the front door was persistent. Claire stood up and walked across the living room and out into the hallway. She saw him then. It stunned her that he was there. He was wearing the blue parka with the zippered pockets and the jeans with the hole in one leg. He had his knapsack slung over his shoulder, and he was waiting for her.

"Oh, Julian," she said through the glass, her voice soft, "you shouldn't have come."

"Please let me in," he said. She could not hear him; she could just see him mouth the words.

For a long minute she did not do anything. She had been

startled by him, and she was not sure what he wanted from her. She opened the door cautiously.

They stood facing each other in the hallway. He did not make a move to touch or kiss her. He stayed perfectly still, watching, and she stared back at him. He seemed to want her to explain herself, and she thought, The nerve of him. He was the one who would have to explain himself, if anyone did. He looked very handsome. Since she had last seen him his hair had grown longer. It now touched the tops of his shoulders.

She remembered a time when they were making love, and he rose up over her, supported by his arms on either side of her, as though he were doing push-ups. His long hair was hanging straight down and grazed her neck and face as he centered himself to find a position where he could watch her. He often did that—stopped everything as though it were a single frame of film, a still. She had been moved by this, by the fact that he wanted to look at her in the middle of making love, that he did not rely solely on some obscure, unrelated visual image in his mind. She had read in a sexual survey in a women's magazine that many men have fantasies during sex that have nothing to do with their partners.

Julian shifted his knapsack to his other shoulder and finally spoke. "Look," he said, "I guess you're probably angry with me for doing this, but I think you should let me explain."

"Okay," said Claire.

"This has been rough on me," he said. His stance had changed slightly; he looked as if he might cry. Claire felt her old, peculiar affection for him. Julian was a good person, and he reached for her in a way that no one ever had before. She had not made herself appear accessible in the past, but this had not mattered to Julian. He had been intrigued by her. She had known it from the start and had been pleased, but still, it put her off. She could not accept such closeness; she needed distance. She needed to see the world through glass.

"I'm sorry," said Claire.

Julian stepped closer. "Claire," he said, "can we talk?"

She didn't move away from him. "All right," she said at last.

They went into the den and Julian sat down on the couch in an oblong of sun. Claire sat in her chair in the far corner, under an eave of shadows.

"I can hardly see you," Julian said. "It's so dark over there."

She remembered the first serious conversation they had ever had, in the dark, up in the stacks of the McCabe library. They had been on equal footing then; he had been in the darkness with her. Now he sat by himself in the light, and she had to concede that it wasn't really fair. She stood up and moved over onto the couch. She sat at the opposite end from him.

"Claire," Julian began when she had settled herself, "I came here for only one reason." He watched her warily; he expected her to resist, to break in and argue at any given moment. "I want to take you out of here," he said. "I've talked this over a lot with Naomi, and she agrees with me that it's the best thing. We both think you've gone too far, and we're worried." He took a breath. "There, that's my whole spiel."

She continued to look at him. The sun picked up all the reddish lights in his blond hair. He sat with his hands in his lap, waiting for her response. "Julian," she said, "you don't understand what's been going on."

"What do you mean?" he asked. "I know exactly what's been going on. I've been talking to Naomi—she's showed me your letters. You're living in Lucy Ascher's house; you're trying to go through what she went through. What more is there?"

Claire shook her head slowly. She told him about the first day at the Aschers', how she had just walked into their lives and stayed. "I'm very important to them," she said quietly. "I remind them of Lucy. I remind myself of Lucy. I'm a death girl, and they need me."

"There is no such thing as a death girl," Julian said, pronouncing each of the words carefully. "I mean it. Death girls don't exist." He told her about Naomi, how she was on the verge of giving up being a death girl, how her dark hair was growing in again. He told her how Laura had become very withdrawn and troubled, and was having some sort of breakdown. Things had changed, he said.

Claire was feeling light-headed. Julian had shown up at the house and disrupted everything. She tried to summon real anger but couldn't. She had begun to feel placid as she sat with Julian. He had come to retrieve her, to whisk her away. People had been doing that to her for years. Was this any different?

She knew suddenly, that it was. She had felt this way one other time in her life, when she had left home for college. It was four in the morning and she stood in her parents' driveway, loading the car. After the last carton had been stowed in the back she realized something: she had outgrown her parents. In a way, she had now outgrown the Aschers. She didn't want to believe it, but there it was, a little revelation.

Julian was watching her closely. "What are you scared of?" he asked in a soft voice.

The sea was making a racket outside. It seemed to Claire that there was no place you could ever go to isolate yourself from the world—there were always peripheral noises, distractions calling you back. There was some irony in this. Claire realized she didn't even like being by herself that much. She was frightened of it, frightened of sinking into sleep all alone. That was how Lucy had been, she knew.

Claire looked at Julian, and her façade quietly collapsed. Something broke, and she wanted to be with him again, back in her bed at school. Her down comforter leaked, and sometimes when they made love, feathers flew out of the split in the seam and gently landed on the two of them. It was like being inside one of those glass paperweights that has a miniature winter scene inside. When you shake it hard, a flurry of snow comes down lightly over the little village, covering rooftops and trees. It would feel nice, being underneath that layer.

"I'm scared of everything," Claire said.

"Me, too," he said, reaching for her.

They both drew back after a moment, and then moved toward each other again. Claire brought her mouth to his, and his lips were warm and ready for her. They stretched out in the length of the sunlight and kissed for a while longer. She ran her hand up under his flannel shirt and easily found the flicker of his heart.

"Claire," he said in a voice from underwater, a voice that implied she was overwhelming him. "Claire."

"Shh," she said, her finger lightly touching his lips. He did not say anything more.

They lay pressed together side by side for half an hour. She played with the fine hair on his arm, moving it back and forth between her fingers, the way she used to. He seemed to shudder as she touched him.

"I guess we have a lot of talking to do," Julian said finally.

"You figured you could just come out here and pick me up," Claire said. "I can't believe it."

"Well, yeah," said Julian nervously, "but I was going to wait a little while before I pressed it."

"I've been thinking of leaving," said Claire. "Even before today. It's always on the edge of my mind. I'll be in the middle of cleaning, and I'll suddenly stop dead and wonder what I'm doing here."

"So you'll come?"

"I guess I will," said Claire slowly. He smiled then, as if her leaving were a coup for him. "I'd better go home first," she added. "I have to face my parents."

They sat up on the couch. Julian's hair fell over his eyes, and she smoothed it back. "I still want to know why you hung up on me," he said.

"That was so long ago," Claire said. "I needed to get away. I'm sorry I acted like that. I don't know what else to tell you."

"Talk to me, Claire," Julian said. "Tell me anything."

As she sat there with him, she began to think of Seth. It was the vulnerability that did it every time. She remembered the day they got very stoned and lay on her parents' couch. She had wanted to save him, and she knew she couldn't.

Afterward she let herself drift into the shadows. She had felt close to him there.

"I had a brother," she said to Julian, and the words came easily, as though it were natural for her to say them. "His name was Seth, and he died when I was fourteen."

She started to talk, telling him random things. She told him about the time Seth and some of his friends had gotten wasted on Boone's Farm Strawberry Hill, and how she took care of him when he threw up—washed out his clothes and put him to bed before their parents came home. "Claire," he had slurred, looking up at her, "you are the best sister in the world. No, I change that. The best sister in the cosmos."

"He always felt like a leftover," Claire told Julian. "He was very sad that he was born too late, that he was too young to have enjoyed the sixties. He wanted to go to Woodstock very badly."

She told him about a photograph she had found in his room after he died. It was a picture of Seth taken at Old Sturbridge Village, with his arms and legs secured in a fake pillory. He was smiling wildly at the camera. "Any time I see people smiling in photographs," she said, "I always wonder what they are smiling about—what they were thinking of at the time."

She talked about her parents, about the stillness and rage that had fallen over her house since the death. She talked about those early days, when she lay in bed and read Lucy Ascher's poetry each morning and evening. "It wasn't even an escape, I guess," she said. "It was the opposite. But there was nothing else I could do." She wondered what kind of person Seth would have become as an adult. Would he have outgrown T-shirts with rock-band logos printed on them? Would he and Claire have remained close? She didn't know.

"Why didn't you tell me any of this before?" Julian asked her.

"I just didn't," Claire said. "You remind me of him; you always have. I couldn't say anything."

The Aschers came home. Claire didn't even hear them come in. She looked up, and they were standing in the entrance to the den, their coats still on. Ray was holding a basket of something in his arms. Their faces were flushed from the outdoors, their noses red. Did they need her anymore? She thought of them dancing in the living room. They had been off in their own world, away from everything else. Helen and Ray's sorrow had moved them together, finally, and she knew that she had been the catalyst. As she looked at them she realized that that was all she had been—the spark, nothing more. You cannot replace children who have died. You can fill in for them for a while, but then you have to step back, gracefully.

Julian stood up and introduced himself, and Helen and Ray shook hands with him. "He's from my college," Claire explained. She did not know what else to say.

They remained in an awkward circle for a few minutes. "We picked these up at a roadside greenhouse," Ray said, fumbling to show them the basket he was holding. They peered down into it. Inside were half a dozen tiny, pearly crocus bulbs. "The first ones of the season," Ray said. "They're kind of premature."

"We'll plant them tomorrow in a pot in the window," Helen said, "and see what happens."

It was Julian who told the Aschers that Claire was leaving. It was later, when they were all sitting around the kitchen table drinking coffee. He said it simply, telling them Claire needed to get back to school, back to her life. Claire could not gauge their response—they nodded after a moment and said they were sorry she was going, but they would not let on more than that. It seemed as though they had been expecting it. I am sitting in Lucy Ascher's chair for the very last time, Claire thought, and she ran her hand along the grain of the arm so that she would always remember what it felt like.

The house was spotless; it had not looked better in a long time. She had slipped so easily into the Aschers' lives, and now she was just as easily slipping out. The speed of things awed her. Ray wrote out a check for the past week's wages, and she gave the Aschers her school address, in case they wanted to keep in touch. Then she went to pack her clothes, leaving Julian downstairs with Helen and Ray. She wondered what they would all find to talk about, what common ground they had. She bunched everything up in her old orange suitcase and stood in the middle of Lucy's room and looked around. It was empty and probably would stay that way.

She was not done with Lucy; chances were that she never would be. She would still lie in her bed at night and recite "Of Gravity and Light" until she had lulled herself to sleep. Sometimes, if she needed to, she would light a bayberry candle and sit cross-legged on her floor until the sun came up. She felt a rush of feeling as she stood in Lucy's room, but it passed quickly. The window was open slightly, and a breeze made the curtains move. She could smell the salt water.

Ray drove them to the train station. They all sat up front because the back seat was loaded with crates of ungraded term papers and examination blue books. Claire looked over her shoulder. Helen was standing on the front porch, watching her go. Some of her hair had come loose and was blowing in her face.

No one talked much during the drive. Claire fiddled with the radio knob until she found some vague music. Drops of rain began to dot the windshield. When they got to the station there was still half an hour until the train was due to arrive. Ray got out and stood under the overhang with them. "I'll wait here with you," he offered.

"We'll be okay," Claire told him. "You might as well go back."

Ray shrugged. "Well, have a good trip," he said, and then he moved away from her and out into the rain. There were no other cars in the parking lot. This was the easiest way for him— passively drifting from a conversation, from a goodbye. He stroked the ragged edges of his beard as he walked to the car. She watched as he got in, hoisting himself onto the seat, yanking the safety belt across the diagonal of his broad chest. He paused and rolled down the window a crack. "Goodbye, Claire," he said softly, and before she could respond he had rolled the window back up and started the engine.

Julian touched her lightly on the shoulder. "Claire," he said.

She turned to him and had to force herself to focus. "I guess

I should call my parents," she said. "What will I say? I hate this kind of thing."

"Just go get it over with," Julian said, and he reached into his pocket and drew out a handful of silver. "Here," he said. "Take what you need."

"Julian the provider," said Claire, and he smiled.

There was a telephone around the other side of the station house. Julian leaned against the brick wall and waited for her. She dropped coins into the pit of the phone. The gears were set in motion, and she was calling home.

"Mom?" she said when her mother answered at last. "It's me."

"Claire." Her mother said her name simply, just a small exhale, the sound of air being released. That was all it took to say her name.

"Mom, I'm coming home," she said as casually as she could but feeling as though she were telephoning from overseas, as though she had been waiting on a long line of soldiers who were all calling their families.

There was a pause, and then her mother said, "I knew you would eventually. That's what I told your father."

"My train gets in at six thirty-eight," said Claire. "Can somebody meet me?"

"I'm in the middle of cooking," her mother said, "and your father is going over to the gym soon." Her voice trailed off. It was the same as always—that admixture of love and stinginess. Her parents could give only so much. Something made them hold back, even at crucial moments. "I guess I could manage to put up the roast and then pick you up," her mother said. "Somehow, I'll be there."

Claire could picture the scene at home. It was a rainy Sunday afternoon, and her father was probably reading one section of the *Times* in the den. Her mother, in the kitchen, was probably reading another. She wondered if she would end up like them—defeated. But she knew, really, that there was a lot more to her parents than defeat. Even when you gave everything up and stopped in your tracks, there were thoughts whizzing through you all day, and all night in the form of dreams. Her parents were caught.

"Goodbye, Mom," Claire said, and she hung up on all that she knew so well—the anger, the hesitance, and most of all the sadness that managed to poke through.

She began to gather her things. The orange suitcase made her feel very young. She had carried it with her everywhere— to visit Joan on the reservation once, to go on a school trip to Washington, D.C., to travel with her family to Europe during that awful summer. Now she was taking it home with her, slightly more worn, the handle taped.

The gates went down, and Claire and Julian walked out onto the platform. She thought about all of the people who traveled by train every day. They always seemed to have a real destination— a home with dinner waiting, a spouse, a parent, a child. She thought of all the embraces some of them would find when they stepped off the train—all the conversations, and later that night all the bed covers that would be turned back, the windows that would be checked, the lights that would be turned off, so that the family could go to sleep, safe under their low roof.

Claire and Julian boarded the train. She would get off at Babylon, and he would continue on into New York. "I'll call you tonight," he said, and she nodded. "I think it will be okay," he added, and even though it was such a broad phrase that it could refer to anything, she was somehow comforted. He was such an optimist. He threw hopeful words out at her indiscriminately, like handfuls of grain, trusting that at least one of the things he said would come true.

"I guess so," she said.

They selected a seat at the end of the car. Claire swung her suitcase onto the rack above her head, then slid across the vinyl seat until she was close to the window. There was an hour's ride ahead of her. Soon she would be home again, where her mother and father waited for her with open, rigid arms.

Meg Wolitzer's novels include *The Wife, The Position, The Ten-Year Nap, The Uncoupling,* and *The Interestings.*

Meg Wolitzer is one of the foremost writers working today. Critically revered, a *New York Times* bestseller as well as book club favorite, she is widely hailed as a master of fiction, writing novels that are simultaneously warm, incisive, funny, provocative, and moving. Wolitzer chronicles the realities of contemporary life with startling perceptiveness and understanding, combining an eye for keen cultural observation with an ear for well-placed humor. She is sharply astute about the feelings and motivations of her characters, but her books are at the same time undeniably novels of ideas.

Whether writing about men, women, families, sex, friendship, and ambition, or grappling with the changing landscape of American life and the fallout of the sexual revolution, Wolitzer addresses serious and complicated themes in ways that make them fresh, riveting, invigorating—and deeply entertaining and satisfying.

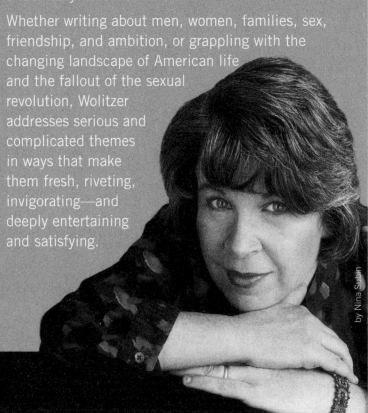

by Nina Subin

T369-1213

THE TEN-YEAR NAP

What happens when smart, educated women temporarily leave the workforce for motherhood—and somehow don't find their way back? This *New York Times* bestselling novel sparked debate among critics, book clubs, and readers everywhere.

For a group of four New York friends the past decade has been defined largely by marriage and motherhood, but it wasn't always that way. Growing up, they were told that their generation would be different. And for a while this was true. They went to

M E G
WOLITZER

The
Ten-Year Nap

New York Times bestselling author of
THE INTERESTINGS

good colleges and began high-powered careers. But after marriage and babies, for a variety of reasons, they decided to stay home, temporarily, to raise their children. Now, ten years later, they are still at home, unsure how they came to inhabit lives so different from the ones they expected—until a new series of events begins to change the landscape of their lives yet again, in ways they couldn't have predicted.

"Wolitzer perfectly captures her women's resolve in the face of a dizzying array of conflicting loyalties. To whom does a woman owe her primary allegiance? Her children? Her mother? Her friends, spouse, community? God forbid, herself?"
—The Washington Post

THE UNCOUPLING

With sly humor and piercing intelligence, *The Uncoupling* looks at love, marriage, and the nature of female desire over time.

When the elliptical new drama teacher at Stellar Plains High School chooses for the school play *Lysistrata*—the comedy by Aristophanes in which women stop having sex with men in order to end a war—a strange spell seems to be cast over the school. Or, at least, over the women. One by one throughout the high school community, perfectly healthy, normal women and teenaged girls turn away from their husbands and boyfriends in the bedroom, for reasons they don't really understand. As the women worry over their loss of passion, and the men become by turns unhappy, offended, and above all, confused, both sides are forced to look at their shared history, and at their sexual selves in a new light.

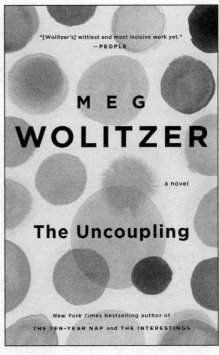

"[Wolitzer's] wittiest and most incisive work yet."
—PEOPLE

M E G
WOLITZER

a novel

The Uncoupling

New York Times bestselling author of
THE TEN-YEAR NAP and THE INTERESTINGS

"Enchanting from start to finish . . . Thoughtful and touching, *The Uncoupling* is also very funny." **—The New York Times Book Review**

THE INTERESTINGS

Wide in scope, ambitious, and populated by complex characters who come together and apart in a changing New York City, *The Interestings* explores the meaning of talent; the nature of envy; the roles of class, art, money, and power; and how all of it can shift and tilt precipitously over the course of a friendship and a life.

The summer that Nixon resigns, six teenagers at a summer camp for the arts become inseparable. Decades later the bond remains, but so much else has changed. Not everyone can sustain, in adulthood, what seemed so special in adolescence. The kind of creativity rewarded at age fifteen is not always enough to propel someone through life at age thirty—not to mention age fifty. Wolitzer follows her characters from the height of youth through middle age, as their talents, fortunes, degrees of satisfaction, and fates diverge.

"*The Interestings* is warm, all-American, and acutely perceptive about the feelings and motivations of its characters, male and female, young and old, gay and straight; but it's also stealthily, unassumingly, and undeniably a novel of ideas. . . . With this book [Wolitzer] has surpassed herself."
—*The New York Times Book Review*

T372-1213

THIS IS MY LIFE

Meg Wolitzer's early novel *This Is My Life* not only firmly established her career, it was also made into Nora Ephron's first film as a director. Originally titled *This Is Your Life* (and changed for the film), it is a smart, witty and perceptive novel about the daughters of a female stand-up comic who watch as their mother struggles to balance her career with the needs of her children.

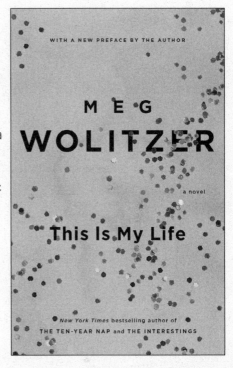

Dottie Engels, comedienne extraordinaire, performs her act in Vegas and on late-night TV. Her two daughters, Opal and Erica, live on the periphery of her glittering life, seeing her on the television screen more often than they do at home. But when Dottie's ratings begin to slide, it takes both her daughters to save Dottie from herself.

This Is My Life expertly captures the uncertainties of adolescence and the trials of growing up in the shadow of a mother who is caught between the conflicting pulls of fame and family.

"There is affection and humor in her voice, and combined with her strong storytelling talents, these qualities lend [*This Is My Life*] both authority and comic warmth."   **—Michiko Kakutani, *The New York Times***